R.L. STINE'S

——— GHOSTS OF ———®

FEAR STREET

HIDE AND SHRIEK

—AND—

WHO'S BEEN SLEEPING
IN MY GRAVE?

TWICE TERRIFYING TALES

ALADDIN
NEW YORK LONDON TORONTO SYDNEY

ALADDIN
An imprint of Simon & Schuster Children's Publishing Division
1230 Avenue of the Americas, New York, NY 10020
This Aladdin paperback edition August 2009
Hide and Shriek copyright © 1995 by Parachute Press, Inc.
Hide and Shriek written by Emily James
Who's Been Sleeping in My Grave? copyright © 1995 by Parachute Press, Inc.
Who's Been Sleeping in My Grave? written by Stephen Roos
All rights reserved, including the right of reproduction in whole or in part in any form.
ALADDIN is a trademark of Simon & Schuster, Inc., and related logo is a
registered trademark of Simon & Schuster, Inc.
FEAR STREET is a registered trademark of Parachute Press, Inc.
For information about special discounts for bulk purchases, please contact
Simon & Schuster Special Sales at 1-866-506-1949
or business@simonandschuster.com.
The Simon & Schuster Speakers Bureau can bring authors to your live event.
For more information or to book an event contact the Simon & Schuster
Speakers Bureau at 1-866-248-3049 or visit our website at www.simonspeakers.com.
Designed by Karin Paprocki
Manufactured in the United States of America
4 6 8 10 9 7 5 3
Library of Congress Control Number 2009928460
ISBN 978-1-4169-9134-2
These titles were previously published individually by Pocket Books.

1209 OFF

HIDE AND SHRIEK

1

"**R**andy! Randy!" My little sister, Baby, wiggled into my room. "Mom says she's going to kill you."

She giggled. She loves to see me get into trouble. Mostly because she's always in trouble herself.

I ignored Baby and yelled down the stairs at my mother. "Stop bugging me, Mom! I'm coming!"

"You're going to be late!" Mom yelled back.

"I know! I can't help it!"

It was my first day at Shadyside Middle School. I didn't want to be late. But I didn't want to show up looking like a dork, either. I'd tried on everything in my closet. Nothing looked right. All my clothes looked babyish on me, which is the last thing I need.

I'm twelve, but people always think I'm younger.

I don't see it, myself. I think I have a very mature face. I am small and wiry. But I'm not *that* small. I wasn't even the smallest girl in the class at my old school.

Some people are so stupid. They don't look at the facts.

I stared at myself in the mirror, tugging at the waist of my jeans. What did the kids in Shadyside wear, anyway? I had no clue. I'd only lived here for two days.

My family—me, Mom, Dad, and my insane little sister—just moved to Shadyside from Maine. We live on Fear Street.

It's a weird name for a street, I think. Fear Street. Not exactly cheery.

Even Shadysiders seem to think the street name is weird. The day we moved in, I went to the post office with Mom, and the clerk gave us a funny look when Mom mentioned our address.

The clerk raised her eyebrows and said, "Fear Street, hmm?"

I thought the clerk was pretty weird herself. She stared at me really hard and then asked how old I was.

"Twelve," I told her.

"Then you might be the one," she commented.

My mom and I exchanged confused glances.

2

"The one what?" I couldn't resist asking.

"You'll find out soon enough—if you aren't careful," she answered mysteriously. "June tenth is right around the corner. You've moved to town at the perfect time."

Yeah, right, I thought. It's great starting a new school at the end of the year. I had to finish the last month of sixth grade in a new school with a bunch of kids I didn't know.

And who didn't know me. And who'll take one look at me today, I thought, and decide right then and there if I'm cool or not.

I yanked off my jeans and tried on my gray jumper again. I wasn't sure it looked good with my brown hair. Mom stormed in.

"Randy, if you try on another stitch of clothing I'll scream. You're wearing that jumper, and that's final."

"Tell her, Mom," Baby said.

I made a face at Baby. She made one back at me.

"Girls!" Mom snapped.

Mom could be tough when she wanted to be. The jumper would have to do. I grabbed my backpack and raced out of the house.

Baby screeched after me, "You're going to be late! You're going to be late! Ha ha ha ha ha!"

Anybody want to adopt a seven-year-old girl?

3

I hurried down Fear Street and around the corner to Park Drive. When I got to Hawthorne, I started running.

Shadyside Middle School loomed ahead. The front doors were closed, and the school yard stood empty. I was definitely late.

Something about the sight of that empty school yard made my stomach flip over. Nervous, I guess. I ran up the steps and tugged on the door.

Locked!

I panicked. Locked out on my first day! Please don't let this be true.

I yanked on the door again. It didn't budge.

I almost burst into tears. What was I going to do?

I told myself to calm down. It can't be locked, I said to myself. They wouldn't lock all the kids inside the school, right? No, they wouldn't.

It helps to think things through like that. Sometimes I get kind of panicky, you know. Carried away by my imagination.

But I also have a sensible side. I can look at the facts. It helps keep my imagination from taking over.

I gave the door one last pull—and this time it flew open. My sensible side was right, I thought. As usual. The door sticks. No reason to get upset.

My footsteps echoed as I stepped into a long,

4

empty hallway. I shifted my backpack and nervously twirled my hair around a finger. I was supposed to report to the principal's office. But I had no idea where it was.

I passed row after row of classroom doors, all closed. Through the doors I heard teachers' voices and the shuffling of chairs. It made the silence of the hallway seem lonelier.

I hope I won't get into trouble for being late, I thought nervously. They wouldn't punish a kid on her first day, would they?

I passed a big bulletin board stuck to one wall. It was covered with announcements and end-of-the-year awards. In one corner someone had tacked a large calendar. It showed the months of May and June, with all the dates x-ed out up to that day, May twenty-second. One date had been circled in red felt-tip—Saturday, June tenth.

I wondered if there was a big game that day. Something about the tenth of June felt familiar. I'd heard something about it somewhere, I knew. The creepy woman in the post office, I remembered. She'd mentioned that date.

Then I noticed a scrawl at the top of the calendar: 18 MORE DAYS UNTIL PETE'S BIRTHDAY. The number was removable so it could be changed as time passed.

Wow, I thought. I wonder who Pete is. He must be pretty popular if the whole school is looking forward to his birthday.

I tore my eyes away from the bulletin board and turned a corner.

"Oh!" I gasped, stopping short. My feet slipped a little on the shiny floor.

A boy staggered toward me. But not a normal boy.

He stumbled forward, clutching his head. His face looked odd—greenish. He must be sick, I thought.

"What's the matter?" I asked. "What happened?"

He moaned in pain. "Help," he croaked. He reached out with bloody hands. Deep red blood oozed from a hideous gash in his head.

I screamed as the boy lurched toward me.

2

"**H**elp!" I cried.

I tried to run, but my feet felt glued to the floor.

The boy fell forward, his hands sticky with blood. I dodged him.

He slumped over, groaning. "My head . . . the pain . . ."

Feeling a little queasy, I bent over the boy. "Are—are you all right?" I asked.

What a stupid question. Blood trickled down his face. Anybody could see he wasn't all right.

The boy groaned louder. A teacher opened her door and stuck her head into the hallway.

"What's all the noise out here?" she demanded.

The bleeding boy suddenly straightened up. "Sorry, Ms. Munson," he said.

He hurried away, looking strangely healthy.

Ms. Munson stared at me. "You—where are you supposed to be?"

"I—I'm new," I stammered. "Where's the principal's office?"

The expression on her face softened a little. "Down this hall and to the right. Welcome to Shadyside!" She shut the door.

I started for the office. What happened to the bleeding boy? I wondered.

I heard a rustling noise, and a tall girl turned the corner and swished toward me. The girl wore a long green dress with a hoop skirt. Her brown hair was tucked under a white lace bonnet.

What a weird school, I thought.

The girl stopped. "Did you see a boy go by?" she asked me. "With blood coming out of his head?"

I nodded. "What happened to him?"

The girl laughed. "Nothing happened to him. It's a costume. We're in the school play, and Lucas plays a guy who gets killed."

"Oh," I said, relieved.

"We have dress rehearsal this morning," the girl said. "I've got to run." She paused. "Are you new? I've never seen you before."

I smiled. "I'm Randy Clay. This is my first day."

"Really?" the girl said. "So you're new. You're *really* new."

"Yes," I answered, confused. "I'm new." What was the big deal?

"Wow, I've got go," the girl said. "I'm late. Nice meeting you, Randy. My name's Sara Lewis. Hope I'll see you later. Bye!"

She ran down the hall, her skirts floating behind her.

I trudged toward the principal's office, shaking my head. What's going on? I wondered. Why is everybody so strange?

I stood outside the door of my sixth-grade class and took a deep breath. I was about to meet the kids who would be my friends from now on—if they liked me. And if I liked them.

I pulled open the door and stepped inside. The teacher, a small young woman with short dark hair, turned away from the blackboard. She smiled at me.

"Miranda Clay?" the teacher asked.

I nodded. "Everybody calls me Randy."

"I'm Ms. Hartman. Welcome. Why don't you take that empty seat in the third row?"

As I started for the empty seat, a buzz arose in the room. The kids stared at me and whispered to one another.

I tried to tell myself not to feel weird about it. They're just wondering who I am, I thought.

I sat next to a pretty girl with wavy blond hair. The girl stared at me, wide-eyed.

"Hi," I said to her.

The girl's eyes grew wider. She turned away from me and whispered to the red-haired girl next to her.

What is it? I wondered. Why are they whispering?

Maybe they're not whispering about me, I thought. I'm probably being too sensitive.

"Let's settle down," Ms. Hartman called.

The whispering gradually stopped.

Ms. Hartman said to me, "You'll be taking final exams during the last week of school. Have you ever taken a final exam before, Randy?"

I shook my head.

"Don't worry. No one else in the sixth grade has, either. Right now we're going over good ways to study and prepare. It's best not to save it until the last minute. . . ."

As the teacher spoke, I glanced around the room. The other kids didn't seem to be paying much attention to Ms. Hartman's study tips. Some of them were staring at me, or stealing glances at me out of the corners of their eyes. The two girls sitting next to me started whispering again.

At last a bell rang and we had recess. Most kids hurried outside. A couple of kids nodded to me and said hi.

"Do you play softball?" a girl asked me as we moved into the hall. She was big, with long dark hair in a braid down her back. A tall blond boy stood beside her.

"A little," I answered.

"We want to set up a coed softball team to play over the summer," the boy explained. He had an easy, friendly smile. I thought he was kind of cute.

"I'm Megan," the girl added. "And this is David."

"Hi," I said.

"I'll go to the gym and borrow a bat," David said. "Maybe we can hit a few during recess."

"Let's wait for him outside," Megan suggested. We stepped out into the bright sunlight.

A few feet ahead of me I noticed the blond girl—Laura—and her friend, Maggie. They turned around. Laura pointed at me.

I tried to ignore them, but it bothered me. What's their problem? I wondered.

"I'll be right back," I told Megan. I hurried inside and ran to the girls' bathroom.

Is something wrong with me? I thought. Have I got something stuck in my teeth? Is my hair sticking up?

I quickly checked myself out in the mirror.

I didn't have a huge pimple on my nose, or big

purple blotches on my cheeks, or a sign on my forehead saying, "Nut case." Nothing like that.

Nothing to explain the way the two girls were behaving.

I hurried back outside. Megan had gathered a bunch of kids together for softball. Sara, the girl I met in the hall, was one of them.

David returned with a bat and ball. "Why don't you play shortstop?" he suggested to me.

I always end up playing shortstop. Is there some rule that shortstops have to be short?

Anyway, I'm good at it from all the practice I get.

Laura and Maggie didn't play softball. They stood on the sidelines and watched.

The next day I saw Sara standing by the big bulletin board in the hall. She had a pen in her hand and was reading a notice on the board.

"Hi," I said. "What's up?"

She smiled. "Hi, Randy." She pointed at the notice she was reading. "I think I might sign up for this."

The notice said: VOLUNTEERS NEEDED TO MAKE PETE'S BIRTHDAY CAKE. SIGN YOUR NAME HERE.

That guy Pete again. I couldn't believe it. People were actually signing up to bake him a cake.

"What is this?" I asked Sara. "Who's Pete?"

"Don't you know?" Sara said. "Well—"

Suddenly I felt a presence behind me. Hot breath on my neck. I jumped and quickly turned around. Sara turned, too.

Laura stood there, reading over our shoulders. She'd crept up behind us so silently we didn't notice her until we felt her breath on our necks.

She glanced at the sign-up sheet. She raised an eyebrow. Then she whispered something to me. It sounded more like a hiss than a whisper.

Could Laura really have said such a mean thing to me?

It sounded as if she'd whispered, "You better watch out!"

3

I wandered through the crowded cafeteria a few days later, looking for Sara or Megan or David. All around me kids shouted, laughed, and joked, filling the room with noise. I relaxed a little.

For once this school feels normal, I thought. All week I've felt like an exhibit in a zoo. Everyone staring at the new girl.

Then I spotted Laura and Maggie. Maggie seemed to be Laura's sidekick or something. I'd never seen her even talking to anyone else.

It was pathetic.

Clutching my tray, I passed Laura and Maggie's table.

"Just wait," Laura murmured. "Just wait until the tenth."

My hands began to shake. This time I knew I hadn't imagined it. Was Laura threatening me?

What would happen on the tenth? I knew June tenth was Pete's birthday. But I still didn't know who Pete was.

I didn't know what to do. My hands shook so hard I was afraid I'd drop my tray in the middle of the lunchroom.

Then I saw someone waving to me from across the room. A skinny boy with curly black hair.

I didn't know who he was. I didn't care. I had to do something—anything.

I wanted to get away from Laura and Maggie as fast as possible. So I hurried toward the boy.

"Hi," he said. "Want to sit with me?"

"Sure," I replied. I still didn't know who the boy was, but he seemed to know me.

"I guess I scared you the other day," the boy said. "Sorry about that. It's like my costume takes over my personality."

I stared at him. What was he talking about?

"By the way," he went on, picking up his sandwich, "my name's Lucas."

Lucas? I thought. It sounded familiar. Oh, yes. Lucas! The boy with the bloody head!

"I'm Randy," I told him. "I didn't recognize you at first. I mean, without blood dripping down your face."

Lucas laughed. "Are you coming to see the play?" he asked me. "It's during the last week of school."

"Sure," I said. "What's it about?"

"It's a Sherlock Holmes mystery," Lucas answered. "The guy who plays Sherlock keeps messing up his lines. You know David Slater?"

"Yeah. He's in my class."

"He's the star of the play," Lucas said. "But he's terrible! I don't know why they picked him."

I opened my brown paper lunch bag and pulled out an apple. I like to eat my dessert first.

"That's too bad," I said between bites. I glanced across the room and caught Laura and Maggie watching me. They quickly turned their heads away.

"So where do you live?" Lucas asked.

"On Fear Street," I replied.

"Really? I live on Fear Street, too. Don't listen to the stories people tell about it. I've lived there all my life, and nothing bad has ever happened to me."

Stories? "What stories?" I asked.

Lucas shrugged. "People tell these crazy stories about Fear Street. Probably because of the name."

"It *is* a creepy name for a street," I admitted.

"You know that cemetery down the road?" Lucas said. "Some kids say it's haunted. My next-door neighbor told me he was riding his bike past there just before dark. He said a tall woman suddenly appeared and blocked his path. But he didn't have time to stop. He slammed on the brakes, but it was too late."

"What happened? Was she hurt?"

"That's the weird part," Lucas told me. "He *says* — if you believe him — that his bike went right through her. As if she were made of air."

"Wow! Was she a ghost?"

Lucas rolled his eyes. "Who knows? I think he was just trying to scare me. *I've* never seen any ghosts around there, myself."

I unwrapped my turkey sandwich but didn't bite into it.

I'm sure Lucas is right, I thought. People just like to tell scary stories.

But I couldn't help feeling uncomfortable. The name Fear Street had to come from something bad that had happened there. Didn't it?

I tilted my head back to catch the sunlight on my face. It felt good to be outside after a long day cooped up in school.

I walked home alone down Hawthorne Drive. My backpack, filled with all my new schoolbooks, hung heavily from my shoulders.

I'll use these books for a month, and then school's over, I thought. It's kind of stupid.

Deep, thick woods stretched out on my right, all

the way to Fear Street, where I lived. I could cut through the woods, I thought. It's probably the quickest way home.

I stepped off the sidewalk and into the woods. Darkness and quiet seemed to fall upon me like a blanket. The warm sunlight vanished.

I suddenly felt chilly. The hair rose on my arms. I rubbed them, shivering.

It's so quiet in here, I thought, glancing around at the tall trees and thick shrubs. No chirps or peeps or animal screeches. Why aren't there any birds or squirrels?

I found a little dirt path that seemed to take me in the right direction. I trudged along the path. The only sound was the crunch of twigs and leaves under my feet.

Crunch, crunch, crunch, crunch.

I walked for ten minutes before the woods began to thin.

I must be getting near the street again, I thought with relief. But I didn't hear the sounds of cars or people.

I came to a large clearing. Slabs of stone rose out of the ground.

Gravestones.

It's a cemetery, I realized.

I felt cold again.

Don't get scared, I scolded myself. The street is

18

on the other side of the cemetery, just beyond the woods. You're almost home.

No big deal, I thought. So you're walking through a cemetery. So what?

Think of the facts. After all, they're only dead people. Dead people can't hurt you. Because they're dead! Right?

I hurried past crumbling stone markers without stopping to read the names on them. I should be almost to my street, I thought.

Still the only sound I heard was the crackle of twigs under my feet. *Crunch, crunch, crunch, crunch.*

But then I thought I heard another sound. A sound I didn't want to hear.

I froze, listening. I scanned the cemetery and the woods beyond. I didn't see anyone. Nothing moved, not even the leaves. I walked on.

Crunch, crunch, crunch, crunch.

Then I heard it again. What was it?

I stopped. Waited. Nothing.

Warily watching the edge of the woods, I took a sideways step.

Something brushed my backpack.

"Oh!" I screamed and wheeled around. I saw a wrinkled old face, laughing at me. An old man.

No—a statue. The statue of a dead old man, sitting on top of his grave.

Laughing like a maniac. Laughing at *me,* I thought.

I've got to get out of here. I picked up my pace, *crunch-crunch-crunch-crunch.*

But I heard it again.

A giggle. Or a laugh.

A boy's laugh.

And footsteps—right behind me!

4

I spun around.

No one there.

I listened. Not a sound.

"I've had enough," I murmured to myself. "Facts or no facts, I'm getting out of here!"

I ran out of the cemetery as fast as I could. I passed through another patch of woods and found myself on Fear Street at last, a few steps away from my house.

I sprinted onto the porch, yanked open the door, and slammed it behind me. I tossed my backpack at the foot of the stairs, safely home. The smell of spaghetti sauce drifted out of the kitchen.

I must have imagined those sounds, I thought.

Maybe I heard an echo of my own footsteps. Or the wind in the trees.

"Randy, is that you?" Mom called from the den. "I'm in here with Baby."

"That's *Barbara!*" my little sister shrieked. "From now on everybody has to call me Barbara! No one is allowed to call me Baby anymore!"

"All right, all right," Mom cooed. "It'll take time to get used to it, that's all."

I found my mother and sister watching cartoons together on the sofa. Mom had changed from her nurse's uniform into dark blue sweatpants and a sweater. She's a little chubby, with long brown hair that she always wears in a ponytail. Baby's pale, knobby knees poked out of short denim overalls.

"I'm seven years old!" Baby hollered at me in her shrill, high-pitched voice. "I'm not a baby anymore!"

"I hear you," I said. "You don't have to yell, Baby."

"BARBARAAAA!!!!" Baby screamed.

"Don't tease her, Randy," Mom scolded. "Could you check the spaghetti sauce for me? Just make sure it's not bubbling over."

"From now on call me Clarissa," I joked as I headed for the kitchen. I lifted the lid on the saucepan. The spaghetti sauce smelled great.

22

"The sauce is fine," I told my mother, settling beside Baby on the couch.

"How was school?" Mom asked me.

"I love my teacher," Baby announced. "His name is Mr. Pine. I'm in love with him!"

"I'm happy for you, Baby, but I'm talking to Randy right now," Mom said.

"That's Barbara!"

"School's okay," I replied. "I've met a lot of nice kids. But a few of them seem weird."

"I'm sure they're nice once you get to know them," Mom assured me.

"I'm going to marry Mr. Pine!" Baby bounced on the couch. "And then I'm going to kiss him!"

"What if he's already married?" I teased.

Baby frowned. "That's impossible. He's mine! Mine mine mine!"

She jumped up and down on the couch like a wild thing. Her shaggy black hair bounced with her. She landed on my thigh.

"Ow!" I cried. "Stop it, Baby! Mom, has she been eating out of the sugar bowl again?"

"Sit down, Baby," Mom commanded. "Look, *Batman*'s on."

Batman was Baby's favorite show. She bounced one last time, landing in a sitting position on the couch.

"My name is *Barbara,*" she insisted. "Everybody has to shut up now. *Batman*'s on."

"Why is she so hyper?" I complained. "She acts like a maniac."

Mom patted my knee. "She's excited because of the move and her new school and everything. She'll settle down."

"No talking!" Baby ordered. *"Batman*'s on!"

"Oh, *please,*" I mumbled, standing up. "I'm going to my room. Call me when dinner's ready."

I picked up my heavy backpack and hauled it upstairs to my room. I dropped the backpack on my desk, kicked the door shut, and flopped onto the bed.

From there I could look out the window. My room faced the street. Across the street stood a bunch of two-story houses a lot like ours. One was painted yellow, another pale blue, another a rusty red-brown.

Beyond those houses I saw the beginning of the woods I had walked through. I couldn't see the cemetery, but I knew it wasn't far away.

You heard the wind in the trees, I told myself firmly. Or a squirrel, maybe.

There's nothing to be afraid of in that cemetery. Nothing to be afraid of at all, I told myself.

Why didn't I believe it?

5

"**H**ey, Randy—catch!"

I turned around. A big leather ball hit me in the stomach.

"Ooof!" I clutched my belly. The ball dropped to the floor.

"Sorry, Randy," Sara called. "I didn't mean to catch you by surprise."

I couldn't answer her right away. She'd knocked the wind out of me.

We were in gym class. Ms. Mason, the gym teacher, had gotten out all this old gym equipment and told us to play with it. I guess she hadn't made a lesson plan for that day.

So Sara had heaved the medicine ball at me. It's

like a beach ball made of lead. Tossing it around is supposed to make your arms strong, I think.

But I was tired that day, and kind of a klutz. If I don't get a good night's sleep, I'm completely brain-dead. And I hadn't slept well since we moved to Fear Street.

"Randy? Are you all right?" Sara looked scared now.

I nodded and straightened up. "I'm okay. Maybe we should play with the hula hoops for a while. They look safe."

Sara grabbed a hot pink hula hoop. I took an orange one. I rocked back on one leg and whirled the hoop around my waist. I frantically swiveled my hips.

Shoop, shoop, shoop. The hoop slipped down to my thighs, my knees, my ankles. The little beads rattled inside it as it hit the floor.

I never could hula hoop.

Meanwhile, Sara *shoop-shooped* away.

"How do you do that?" I asked.

"It's easy," she said with a shrug. "You just do it."

I picked mine up and tried again.

Shoop, shoop, shoop, clatter. Straight down to the floor.

"You want to come to my house this Saturday?"

Sara asked me as she hula'd. "I'm having a sleepover."

I was so happy I almost shouted my answer. "Sure! That would be great!"

Maybe at the sleepover I'd get to know some other girls, and soon I'd have a whole crowd of friends.

Laura shimmied past me then, twirling a baton. "Better get in shape, Randy," she murmured. "Or else find a good place to hide."

I glanced at Sara. Her eyes widened.

"*She's* not going to be at your sleepover, is she?" I asked.

"No," Sara replied.

"Good," I said. "What is she talking about? She said something like that to me last week. Why is she always telling me to watch out?"

Sara let her hula hoop clatter to the floor.

"It's hard to explain, Randy."

"What do you mean, 'it's hard to explain'? Can't you give me a hint, at least?"

I hadn't meant to be funny, but Sara laughed.

"All I mean is it's a long story," she answered. "You'll find out more on Saturday."

I pressed on. "Tell me this much. Am I in some kind of trouble?"

Sara shook her head. "No more than anyone else, Randy. At least I don't think so."

27

Gym class finally ended. Sara and I changed and went to art class. We went to teachers besides Ms. Hartman for a couple of subjects.

We sat at a table with Megan and David and molded wet gray blobs of clay into bowls and cups and saucers.

"Is this play going to be any good, you guys?" Megan asked. "Sherlock Holmes sounds kind of boring to me."

"It's going to be great," Sara told us. "Everyone in it is really good—don't you think, David?"

"Yeah," David agreed, smoothing out the lines of a mug he was making. "Except for Lucas. He's a ham."

"I think Lucas is pretty good," Sara said. She poked dots around the rim of a saucer. "Anyway, his part isn't very big. Basically he gets stabbed by the killer and then lies there while you check out the scene for clues. Playing a corpse should be easy enough for Lucas. How bad could he be?"

"I saw Lucas in his makeup," I put in. "He almost scared me to death."

"He's terrible," David insisted. "All that moaning and shaking. He practically wrecks the play."

"Come on, David," Megan scoffed. "He can't be that bad."

"Okay, he's not that bad," David admitted. "But he's still the worst thing in the play."

"That's probably why he has the smallest part," Sara said.

We all laughed. I felt happy. My second week at school, and I already had some friends. And Sara's sleepover was only two days away.

Sara lived in a big brick house in North Hills. Dad parked out front and went inside with me to meet the Lewises.

My dad's tall and dark-haired and athletic. He wears ugly black-rimmed glasses, but I think he's handsome anyway. He wears jeans and tweed jackets and looks like a professor, but he's really a computer programmer.

Mr. and Mrs. Lewis led us into the living room. Some other parents were sitting there, drinking coffee.

"Welcome to Shadyside," Mrs. Lewis said when she shook Dad's hand. She was tiny and neat. She looked funny next to her husband, who was as tall as Dad. "Sara tells me you just moved here from Maine."

Mr. Lewis handed Dad a cup of coffee and turned to me. "Why don't you take your things down to the basement, Randy? The other girls are already getting settled down there."

Dad leaned over to kiss me goodbye. "Look out for the octopus," he whispered.

He was thinking of the first time I went to a friend's house to sleep over. My friend Tanya's house.

Tanya had weird parents. They served us octopus for dinner.

When Tanya and I got into bed, I kept thinking about the octopus. I felt sure the dead octopus's tentacles were going to reach out from under the bed. They'd grab me and the octopus's ghost would get its revenge by eating me.

I started crying. I called my parents and begged them to come and take me home. Tanya thought I didn't like her anymore.

I was only seven years old at the time. That was before I'd decided not to let my imagination run away with me. Before I realized you have to look at the facts.

You'd think Dad would have forgotten about it by now. I wished he'd let *me* forget it.

"Very funny, Dad," I sniffed.

I carried my sleeping bag through the kitchen and down to the basement.

"Randy's here!" Sara called as I came down the steps.

Our basement is like a dungeon, but the Lewises was all fixed up with a TV and VCR, a stereo, even a kitchenette in one corner. The floor was carpeted,

30

and travel posters covered the walls. Nothing scary about this basement at all.

Sara introduced me to the other girls: Megan, Anita, Karla, and her twin sister, Kris.

I already knew Megan, of course. And I'd seen Anita in gym.

"Spread out your sleeping bag," Sara said. "We're going to make popcorn and watch a horror movie."

I searched for a spot for my sleeping bag. At slumber parties your sleeping-bag spot can be a big deal. Back in Maine, Tanya and I always put ours next to each other.

The other girls had already spread their sleeping bags out over the carpet. Kris and Karla zipped theirs together to make it a double. The sleeping bags formed a rough semicircle in front of the TV. I unrolled my bag in the middle.

Sara made popcorn in the microwave. Mrs. Lewis appeared at the foot of the stairs.

"Having fun, girls?" she asked. "I won't bother you anymore, but you know where to find me if you need me. Don't stay up too late, ha ha."

"Right, Mom," Sara said.

"And try not to make *too* much noise. Sara's little brothers will be going to bed soon. If they can't sleep, I'm going to send them down here to play with you. And I *know* you don't want that."

"She's bluffing," Sara said.

"I am not," her mother replied. "Well, good night, girls. Have a good time!" She waved and tapped her way upstairs in her high-heeled shoes.

"Your mother's so nice, Sara," Kris said.

Sara rolled her eyes. "You should hear her when I come home late."

We all giggled. The timer on the microwave went off, and soon Sara set a big bowl of popcorn beside me.

"What movie are we going to watch?" I asked.

"Dracula," Sara answered.

Kris groaned. "Do we have to watch a scary movie? I get scared really easily."

"You can go upstairs and hang out with my mother if you want," Sara teased. "Since you're so crazy about her."

"Kris, you moron," Karla said. "We already saw *Dracula,* and you said it wasn't scary at all!"

"Oh, yeah. I forgot." Kris smiled sheepishly. She seemed like a nice girl, but kind of spacey. She and Karla looked exactly alike—round faces, big dark eyes, ski-jump noses—except that Karla wore her frizzy black hair short, and Kris kept hers in two thick braids. So far that was the only way I could tell them apart.

We put on our pajamas and settled into our

sleeping bags. Sara slid the tape into the VCR and turned out the lights.

The movie began. It was an old black-and-white version of *Dracula.* I think black-and-white movies are scarier than color—they're so shadowy and dark.

Dracula sank his fangs into his victims' necks. The hair prickled on the back of mine. "It's not real blood," I told myself. "It's only chocolate syrup."

When the movie ended, Sara didn't turn on the lights. We sat and talked in the glow of the television set. The screen showed nothing but fuzz and static now.

"That wasn't scary at all," Kris declared.

"Oh, right," Karla countered. "And you didn't dig your fingernails into my arm the whole time." She flashed her forearm, showing us the marks her sister's nails had made.

"Dracula's not as scary as Pete," Anita said.

The room went quiet all of a sudden. I had that feeling, the feeling I'd had ever since I moved to Shadyside—that everyone knew something I didn't.

I broke the silence. "Who's Pete?"

No one answered.

6

"**W**ho's Pete," I asked again. "Is that the guy with the hockey mask?"

Everybody laughed. But it sounded sort of phony.

"Pete's not a character in a movie," Anita told me. "He's *real.*"

"Real?" I said. "Who is he?"

No one answered right away. The other girls glanced at each other. They wouldn't look me in the eye.

They're just trying to scare me, I told myself. Don't panic. Wait for the facts.

"The tenth is almost here," Kris whispered. "One week from tonight."

The tenth! Not that again.

"What's going on?" I demanded. "What's happening on the tenth?"

Silence.

"Why won't anybody tell me?" I wailed.

Still the girls kept quiet. I watched their faces in the gray-blue light of the TV.

"She'll have to find out sooner or later," Anita said.

"Tell me," I insisted.

"It's not fair to keep it from her," Kris said.

Another silence. Sara stood up and got a candle. She lit it and placed it on the floor in the middle of the semicircle. She switched off the TV.

Then Anita spoke.

"Pete was a boy who lived in Shadyside a long, long time ago," she said in a low voice. "He died on his twelfth birthday. He died in the Fear Street Woods."

The candlelight flickered across the girls' faces. They had probably heard the story of Pete a thousand times before, I guessed, but it still held them spellbound.

"No one knows how he died," Anita went on. "His body was found one morning, all shriveled up.

"His parents gave him a funeral. They buried him in the cemetery. They thought that was the end of Pete.

"But one year later—one year to the day after

35

Pete died—some kids were playing hide-and-seek in the Fear Street Woods. All of a sudden a girl started screaming.

" 'It's Pete!' she shrieked. 'I saw Pete!'

"The kids ran screaming out of the woods. Pete had been playing hide-and-seek with them."

Anita paused for a long moment.

"One boy left that game completely changed. He began to stay up late at night, howling like an animal. He ran off by himself into the woods. No one knew what he did there. But they knew the boy was not the same.

"Exactly one year later the boy seemed to snap out of it. He stopped going out at night. He stopped going outside at all. He was too scared.

"The boy stayed in bed all day, shaking. His eyes never blinked—he held them wide open all the time, as if he were always terrified. And overnight his hair had turned from dark brown—to white. He looked like an old man.

"A doctor came to examine him. The boy told the doctor that Pete tagged him in the game. And then got to control his body every night. For one year Pete had made the boy do these gross, disgusting things. Pete even made the boy sleep in the cemetery sometimes! Then Pete left.

"No one believed the boy, of course. But then the

36

same thing happened to another kid in town. And the next year, another.

"People began to get scared. Soon no children were ever allowed to play in the Fear Street Woods. But that didn't stop Pete.

"The next year, when no children came to play hide-and-seek on Pete's birthday . . . Pete got angry.

"Pete got very angry. And bad things started to happen. One girl looked in the mirror and saw her face rotting away. Her skin was all green and her teeth were black.

"Another kid kept smelling something, something so putrid that he couldn't eat. Every time he tried, he would gag. He kept getting thinner and thinner.

"Some kids' pets disappeared. Some kids heard a boy yelling 'Ready or not, here I come' over and over until they almost went crazy.

"No one could say for sure that Pete caused the bad things to happen. But they stopped when the kids finally returned to the woods for the game."

Anita stared at Randy with a serious expression on her face.

"Now, every year on the tenth of June, we all celebrate Pete's birthday. We go into the Fear Street Woods and play hide-and-seek. Pete is It.

"The first person Pete tags is the loser. Pete takes over his body for the rest of the year. That kid has to watch while Pete does whatever he wants every single night.

"Pete wants a body to live in. A real, live body. He doesn't want to be a ghost. He wants to be alive. Every year he takes a new kid's body. This year it's going to be one of *us!*"

Not one of us moved. I watched the candlelight play on Anita's face. Maybe she was pretending. But she looked scared.

It's just a story, I thought to myself. It has to be.

And I thought Pete was some super-popular kid at Shadyside Middle School!

Sara broke the silence. "That's what the legend says, anyway."

Everyone stared at me, waiting for my reaction.

"Wow," I said. "Um, that's a good story, I guess."

"It's true," Anita insisted. "On June the tenth Pete is going to tag someone we know. Maybe one of us."

"I hope it's not me," Kris said. "I heard Pete makes you run through the woods all night long. He keeps you up all night so you're really tired the next day."

Kris was such a ditz. Karla gave her a punch on the shoulder.

"That's not so scary," I commented.

38

"Well, *I* heard he kills animals and eats them," Sara said. "Remember that time Jeff Walker's dog disappeared? A lot of people thought Pete got him."

"Eeeeyeeew." I was starting to feel a little sick.

Anita pulled a strand of her brown hair out of her mouth. I could tell she believed in Pete and was afraid of him. "He goes to the cemetery at night. And the Fear Street Woods. He howls like an animal. He becomes wild."

"When our grandfather was a kid, his best friend got tagged," Kris told me. "When the year was over, he went crazy. He ended up in an insane asylum."

Karla rolled her eyes. "Only you would fall for Grandpa's old stories, Kris."

"It's true!" Kris insisted.

"My older sister played a few years ago," Anita put in. "She said that after the game this one girl's hair turned completely white, just like in the legend. She looked like a little old lady."

"I heard about a boy who stopped talking completely," Sara said. "Pete took over his body, and the boy never said another word. He just wandered the streets. His jaw shook and his eyes rolled around in his head. He never recovered.

"The things Pete made him do were so terrible . . ." Anita added. "So horrible, he couldn't talk about it. He couldn't talk at all."

39

How awful, I thought. Panic rose in my throat. But I pushed it down.

Facts, I told myself. These are just stories. You need facts.

Megan touched my arm and looked me straight in the eye now. "The thing is, Randy . . . you're in more danger than the rest of us."

That prickly feeling on the back of my neck returned. "I am? Why?"

She leaned forward and whispered in a strange, low voice, "Because Pete likes new kids. That's why."

The candle flickered, then went out.

A scream cut through the darkness.

7

The basement went pitch-black.

We all huddled together, clutching one another and screaming.

Then, through the screaming, I thought I heard laughter.

Sara must have heard it, too. She said, "Joseph? Paul? Is that you?"

She crawled to a side table and fumbled for the light switch.

The light came on. Against the wall by the stairs crouched two little boys in feetie pajamas. They slumped over, laughing.

"I should have known," Sara huffed. "It's only my stupid little brothers."

They giggled as she chased them up the stairs.

"Just wait till your Cub Scout sleepover!" she shouted after them. "You're going to be sorry! You're going to wish you'd joined the Camp Fire Girls!"

She returned to the semicircle of sleeping bags, scowling.

"Don't yell at them, Sara," Kris said. "I think your little brothers are adorable."

"You can have them," Sara answered. "Take them and Mom, too."

"Should we watch another movie?" Karla asked. "Or maybe there's something good on TV."

"Wait a second," I cut in. "I want to hear more about Pete."

"It's just an old story, Randy," Sara assured me. "You don't have to worry. We were just trying to scare you." She paused. "Right, everybody?"

No one said a word. Anita's big blue eyes watched Sara a little fearfully.

"A-neee-ta," Megan teased. "Only one more week to go."

"People don't tell all these stories about Pete for no reason," Anita insisted. "They're true. I'm sure they are."

"Come on, Anita," Karla said. "You'll believe anything. Remember that time Megan told you her teeth were really dentures? You fell for it!"

Anita's eyes flashed, but she blushed.

"Stop teasing Anita," Sara said. "If you don't believe in Pete, Karla, why are you playing in the game?"

"Why would *anybody* play this game?" I demanded. "That's the part I don't get. I mean, if there's really a ghost named Pete who could take over your body, why take a chance?"

Kris flashed me her dippy smile. "Because it's fun."

"It's not that scary," Megan insisted. "It's kind of cool. Like going to a haunted house on Halloween. You hear about it from the older kids when you're little, so you look forward to it. When you're old enough to play, you get to scare the little kids with it."

"Everybody talks about it afterward," Karla said. "Creepy things happen in the woods, but funny things, too. I'd hate to miss it."

"And if you don't play," Kris added, "everybody thinks you're a wimp."

"You have to play, Randy," Sara said. "Everybody plays."

The other girls laughed.

"Watch out, Randy," Megan murmured. "Pete is going to choose you!"

Karla giggled. "Don't forget—Pete likes new kids, Randy."

43

"You better practice running," Kris added. "You have to run pretty fast to get away from a ghost."

They all giggled, teasing me and poking me. I pretended to laugh along. But inside I felt worried —and scared.

It's just a game, I told myself. An old tradition.

But what if there were more to it?

"If this legend is true," I began, "that means Pete must be living in some kid's body now. Right? Maybe somebody we know!"

"That's right, Randy," Megan taunted. "Pete could be sitting next to you in school."

"Or in this very basement!" Kris added.

"It could be me!" Sara cried.

"Or me!" Karla said.

"Or me!" Megan shouted, grabbing me.

I yelped. The other girls laughed.

"Randy, watch out! Pete's right behind you!"

Karla pointed and pretended to look scared. The other girls cracked up.

Is any of this true? I wondered. Or are they just trying to scare me?

Facts. That's what I needed.

Cold, hard facts.

I'm going to investigate, I decided.

I'm going to find out the truth.

* * *

At school on Monday all I could think about was Pete. And the hide-and-seek game coming up. I passed the bulletin board. More days were x-ed out. Five more days to Pete's birthday.

I kept remembering the stories I'd heard at Sara's sleepover. About how Pete takes somebody's body and uses it at night to do weird, gross things.

Whoever's body he uses, I figured, must be pretty tired all day. I stared into kids' faces, looking for circles under their eyes.

It turned out a lot of kids at Shadyside Middle School looked a little tired. I don't know what *they* were doing all night.

Worrying about Pete, maybe?

I noticed Laura and Maggie glancing around warily. Maybe they're trying to figure out whose body Pete lives in, too, I thought. Laura sneered when she saw me. "You're doomed, new girl," she called.

At least now I knew what she was talking about.

At lunchtime I threaded my way through the crowded halls to my locker. I needed to get my lunch bag.

From halfway down the hall I saw a tall, skinny boy leaning against my locker. Who's that? I wondered.

I think I might need glasses. I don't see too well from far away.

I moved a little closer.

Lucas.

What's he doing? I wondered, approaching my locker. Is he waiting for me?

Why would he be waiting for me? I thought nervously. What does he want?

I took a deep breath and strode over to my locker. He noticed me and straightened up. He *was* waiting for me.

"Hi, Randy."

"Hi, Lucas." I busied myself with my combination lock. I missed the second number and had to start over again.

"Going to lunch now?" he asked.

He leaned against the locker next to mine. He watched me fumble with my lock. He made me nervous. I messed up the combination again.

"Um, yeah," I answered absently. What was my combination again? Twenty-three, five . . .

"So, you want to eat lunch with me?"

I dropped the lock, still unopened.

I studied Lucas's face. Deep blue circles rimmed his eyes.

He looked awfully tired.

"I just thought you might want someone to eat with, since you're new and all. . . ." he added.

The hairs prickled on the back of my neck. *"Pete likes new kids,"* everybody said.

46

Lucas didn't give up. "Are you going to the hide-and-seek game on Saturday? I really hope you'll be there."

Alarms went off in my head. They started out as tiny clock-radio alarms and grew louder until it sounded like a squadron of police sirens in my brain.

"You have to go," Lucas insisted. "Everybody goes."

Why is it so important to him? I wondered in a panic.

What does he care whether I, the new girl, go to the hide-and-seek game?

I could only think of one reason.

Oh, no, I thought.

Lucas is Pete!

8

Calm down, I told myself.

I leaned my head against my locker and concentrated on the lock. Twenty-three, five, seventeen. Click. The lock opened.

"So, how about it, Randy?" Lucas persisted. "Want to eat with me?"

Don't get him angry, I said to myself. Stay calm—and stay away from him.

I dumped my books in the bottom of my locker. "I can't," I told him.

"Oh. Okay." He drooped a little.

"I promised David and Sara I'd go over the math homework with them," I explained.

Well, it was true.

"David Slater?" Lucas straightened up. "He's such a jerk."

"No, he's not," I said. "He's very nice."

"We'll eat together tomorrow, then," Lucas insisted. "Right?"

"Well—" I hesitated.

"Right, Randy?"

"Sure," I agreed queasily. "Tomorrow."

I watched him slowly walk down the hall toward the lunchroom. A little shiver raced through me. Does the Pete inside him want to tag *me* in the Fear Street Woods?

Stop, I ordered myself. Consider the facts. One: Lucas looks tired. Two: He seems to like me—the new kid. Three: He wants me at the hide-and-seek game.

But that's not enough to prove Lucas is Pete. I'm going to find out for sure, I decided. If I'm positive that Lucas is Pete, I can avoid him at the game.

I won't let him catch me. I don't want to spend the next year with a disgusting boy ghost. Or any ghost at all.

I grabbed my lunch and hurried off to meet David and Sara. I found Sara at a corner table in the back of the cafeteria.

"David's in line getting ice cream," Sara explained.

"Listen, Sara," I said breathlessly. "You've got to help me."

"Help you what?"

"I think Pete has taken over Lucas's body. I'm going to spy on him until I find out for sure. Will you help me?"

Sara stared at me as if I'd gone crazy. "Lucas?" she cried. "No way."

"I think so," I insisted. "You know what he did? He asked me if I'd eat lunch with him."

Sara slapped her hands against her cheeks in mock horror. "He asked you to eat *lunch* with him? That's terrifying!"

I sighed impatiently. *"Listen.* Then he said something about me being *new.* And *then* he said he hoped I'd be at the hide-and-seek game! Plus he looks tired—probably from staying up all night in the graveyard!"

Sara tapped her chin. "I don't know, Randy. It sounds kind of silly to me. I mean, I'm not even sure I believe in all this Pete stuff. We were just trying to scare you at the sleepover."

I wasn't sure I believed in Pete, either. But if there was nothing to the stories, why had they lasted all these years? Why were some kids, like Anita, truly afraid of him? I had to find out— *before* the game.

I nudged Sara. "You won't help me?"

"Help you what?" David sat down, slurping on an ice-cream cone.

"Randy wants to spy on Lucas. She thinks he's Pete."

David laughed. "Lucas? No way."

"That's what I said," Sara pointed out.

I turned to David. "I want to find out for sure, and Sara won't help me. And—well, it would be kind of scary to spy on Lucas alone. Will you help me, David?"

David gaped at me as if I'd lost my mind.

"Come on, David," I pleaded. "It makes sense! If we know who Pete is before the game, we can stay away from him. And you don't want him to tag you, do you?"

"No, I don't," David said. "But what if he catches us spying on him?"

"He won't," I assured him. "We'll be extra extra careful. Please, David?"

He glanced at Sara, who shook her head as if to say, "Randy is nuts and we might as well accept it."

"Okay," David said. "I'll help you."

"Thanks!" I felt better already. "When should we start?"

David shrugged. "How about tonight?"

"You guys are crazy," Sara declared.

"Maybe," I replied. "But when June tenth comes, David and I will know who to hide from. Who knows, Sara—maybe Pete will tag *you.*"

I waited until after dinner, when darkness approached.

"I'm going out for a walk around the neighborhood," I told Mom and Dad.

"Can I come?" Baby squealed.

That's just what I need, I thought. Baby tagging along. No way.

"You can't come," I told her firmly. "I want to be alone."

"Be careful, honey," Mom said. "Don't stay out too long."

"I won't," I promised, pushing open the kitchen door.

But secretly I thought, I'll stay out as long as it takes.

I met David on the corner of Fear Street and Park Drive.

"You ready?" he asked.

"Ready," I replied.

We walked to Lucas's house.

Lucas lived on Fear Street, too, not far from my house. We stood across the street, hiding in the shadows. There were lights on in Lucas's kitchen. I saw a woman in the window.

"Who's that?" I whispered.

"Looks like Lucas's mother," David said. "Washing the dishes or something."

We waited. So far the only movement was Lucas's mother in the kitchen window. This could get pretty dull, I thought.

"What if Lucas doesn't come out?" I asked. "What if we waste the whole night standing here for nothing?"

"Shh!" David whispered. "Look!"

The front door opened. Lucas appeared. He hurried down the steps and across the front lawn. He started down Fear Street, toward the woods.

David and I ducked behind a parked car until he passed. Then we followed him. We stayed on the other side of the street. I prayed he wouldn't notice us.

He walked briskly down the street, whistling. The tune sounded familiar.

What *is* that song? I wondered. I know it from somewhere.

He whistled it over and over. At last I recognized it. I remembered singing it as a little kid.

A funeral march. The words went:

Pray for the dead, and the dead will pray for you,
Simply because there is nothing else to do.

53

I glanced at David. He knew the song, too.

"Creepy," I whispered. "Why is he whistling a funeral march?"

"Maybe it's Pete," David suggested. "Remembering his own funeral."

I shivered.

We passed by my house. I glanced at it longingly. So warm and cozy and safe. Maybe I should run back inside and forget all about this, I thought.

But Lucas kept walking. And David did, too. It was nice of David to come with me. I couldn't let him down now.

And anyway, I had to find out the truth about Lucas.

We reached the Fear Street Woods. Lucas turned off the road and disappeared into the trees.

David and I crossed the street. We hesitated at the edge of the woods.

"It's awfully dark in there," I said.

I heard Lucas's footsteps crunching over the twigs and leaves. They moved deeper and deeper into the woods, and farther away from us.

"We're losing him!" David exclaimed. He started into the dark, dark woods.

My feet didn't seem to want to follow. But I forced them. I didn't want to be alone.

We listened for Lucas's footsteps, trying to follow them.

54

"This way!" David whispered. We shuffled through the shrubs.

But Lucas's footsteps grew faint. After a few minutes I didn't hear a sound.

Where did he go?

I wanted to call out, "Lucas! Where are you!" But I knew that would be stupid. I didn't want him to find us.

We stumbled through the woods, trying not to make noise.

No sign of him now. Lucas had disappeared. He was lost in the shadows.

Then I heard noises off in the distance. I listened hard.

"David! Do you hear that?"

He froze, listening.

It sounded like kids' voices. Kids' voices shouting something.

A breeze fluttered the leaves. The sounds grew clearer, carried on the wind.

I thought I heard a shout of, "Olly olly oxen free!"

There were giggles, and then, "You're It! You're It!"

What's going on? I wondered.

Maybe it's Pete. Maybe he's practicing for the hide-and-seek game!

"I tagged you! You're It!"

I shivered in my shorts and T-shirt. It's June, I

thought. I shouldn't be cold. But the breeze blew across my skin. The hair on my arms stood straight up.

A childish voice screamed, "Run home! Run home!"

David grabbed me by the arm. Sweat dripped down his face. "We've got to get out of here!" he cried.

He yanked on my arm. I didn't have a chance to say a word. We tore through the woods as fast as our sneakers would take us. I could barely keep up with David.

A little boy began to chant. "Five . . . ten . . . fifteen . . ."

"Come on, Randy!" he shouted. "Hurry up!"

I think he was even more scared than I was.

The Fear Street Woods loomed around us like a pitch-black maze. I dodged trees and branches, trying to keep up with David.

"Forty-five . . . fifty . . . fifty-five . . ." the boy called.

Please don't let Lucas spot us, I begged. Please let us get out of here okay.

"This way!" David cried. He pointed to a light up ahead.

"Seventy . . . seventy-five . . . eighty . . ." The boy's voice grew higher and shriller.

I didn't know what the light was. I hoped it meant safety. I aimed my body at it and pumped my legs as hard as they could go.

As I ran, I heard the little boy cry, "One hundred! Ready or not, here I come!"

9

The light swerved past. A car's headlights. It led us safely out of the woods.

David and I stood panting on the curb. Then David started chuckling. A few seconds later he was laughing his head off.

"What's so funny?" I demanded.

David gulped air, trying to catch his breath. "Us!" he gasped. "We got scared of a bunch of little kids!"

He's right, I realized. We heard a bunch of kids playing in the woods and ran out of there screaming bloody murder.

"I'm glad none of our friends saw us!" I said, laughing with him. "We'd never live it down!

"Help! Help! It's a bunch of little kids!"

David pretended to scream. "Oh, no! It's a first grader!"

"Look out!" I joked. "He's got finger paint on his hands!"

"We're too jumpy," David said. "Pete probably doesn't even exist."

"Yeah," I agreed. "We let a stupid story scare us silly."

But inside I wasn't so sure.

The next day Lucas waited by my locker again. Luckily I saw him ahead of time. I turned around and walked in the other direction.

My lunch sat in my locker, guarded by Lucas.

I patted my pockets as I hurried away, wondering if I had any change.

Fifty cents. Enough for an ice-cream sandwich.

I didn't mind. It was better to skip lunch than end up eating raw animals every night.

"Randy, you're starting to scare me," Sara whispered.

"I have to know for sure," I murmured.

We were all gathered on the bleachers in the gym, boys and girls together. Sara and I sat with Kris and Karla.

"Why else would Lucas go into the woods at night?" Sara said. "Either he's Pete, or he's up to something strange. You ought to stay away from him, Randy."

"But I still don't have enough *facts.* Lucas might not be Pete—and I need to know one way or the other before the game. It's only three days away now."

"What are you guys whispering about?" Kris asked.

"Nothing," Sara replied.

"Why won't you tell—" Kris whined.

"What do you think is happening?" Karla interrupted her sister. "We never have gym with the boys."

Usually the girls had gym by themselves. The boys had their own gym teacher, Mr. Sirk.

"I bet we're going to learn judo or something," Kris guessed.

"Like self-defense?" I asked.

"Yes!" Kris's voice rose in excitement. "Maybe we'll learn how to flip the boys over! Wouldn't that be excellent?"

"If only," Karla murmured. "But I can't imagine Ms. Mason teaching us self-defense."

Ms. Mason wore an awful lot of makeup for a gym teacher. Her nails were bright red and always perfectly manicured. If you threw a ball to her, she wouldn't catch it. She'd just let it go—and make

60

you chase it. I guess she was afraid of chipping a nail.

She was careful about her hair, too. She dyed it white-blond and must have used gallons of hairspray on it because it poofed around her head and never moved. She didn't like to go outside on windy days.

She seemed to have other things on her mind besides teaching gym to twelve-year-olds.

"Okay, everybody," she called out, clapping her hands together lightly.

"I think Ms. Mason has a crush on Mr. Sirk," Kris whispered to me.

Mr. Sirk had a weight lifter's build, a head of wavy, glossy dark hair and a mustache. He liked to walk around with his chest puffed out. Mr. Sirk whispered something to Ms. Mason. Ms. Mason giggled.

"See?" Kris gloated.

"Gross," I said.

Ms. Mason clapped her hands again. "I guess you're wondering why the boys and girls are having gym together this week. Well, I'll tell you. We'll be learning something new and different."

"If not judo, then karate," Kris wished aloud. "Please, please, please!"

"Something I think you'll all enjoy," Ms. Mason went on. "Square dancing!"

We all groaned.

Mr. Sirk blew his whistle. "Hey! Let's quiet down now!" he cried sharply.

We quieted down.

Ms. Mason said, "I know you're all excited, but you won't learn anything if you keep talking."

She paused. "Mr. Sirk and I will demonstrate the steps. Then we'll put on a tape of real country music, and you all can try it yourselves. Mr. Sirk himself will be the caller!"

Ms. Mason seemed to think this was very exciting news. No one in the sixth grade got worked up about it.

"First of all, you'll need to choose partners. If you have somebody in mind, go ahead and choose him or her. If you don't have a partner, we'll match you up with somebody."

No one moved, but everyone started talking.

"This should be good," Karla commented.

"I'll bet you anything Laura picks David," Kris said. "You watch."

But no one made a move to pick anyone. Ms. Mason clapped her hands for the zillionth time.

"If you don't want to choose your own partners, Mr. Sirk and I will be happy to choose for you."

"I don't care who I'm with, as long as it's not Jeff Fader," Karla declared. "He's so gross."

Karla, Kris, and I all leaned forward to peek at

Jeff Fader. He sat in the front row of bleachers, picking his nose.

"Yuck!" Kris cried.

Suddenly, from behind us, a girl's voice rang out. "I choose David Slater!"

I turned around. It was Laura.

"What did I tell you?" Kris crowed.

David slumped down on the bleacher and turned dark red. The boys around him slapped him on the back, laughing.

Ms. Mason shouted, "That's the spirit, Laura! Thanks for getting things started. David, you and Laura can come down onto the gym floor. Anyone else?"

For a few seconds no one said a word.

"No one wants to do this dumb square-dancing thing," Karla whispered. "Why doesn't Ms. Mason give up?"

Then, from the middle of the crowd, Lucas shot up.

"I choose Randy Clay!" he called.

10

Lucas chose me!

This time no one laughed or clapped. The bleachers stayed quiet. Kris and Karla stared at me with twin pairs of wide eyes.

From down on the gym floor, David gave me a meaningful look.

Pete likes new girls, they said.

Pete's going to choose *you*.

Lucas chose me.

The facts were adding up.

"All right, Lucas!" Ms. Mason called. "Randy, where are you? Randy is the new girl, right?"

I sat glued to my bench, my legs shaking.

I didn't want to be Lucas's partner. I didn't even

want to learn how to square-dance. But that was beside the point.

"What am I going to do?" I whispered to Kris and Karla.

Karla shrugged. "I guess you'd better go out there."

Lucas made his way down to the gym floor.

"Randy!" Ms. Mason called. "Oh, Randy! I know you're up there somewhere. Come down so we can get things started."

Laura's friend Maggie stood up and pointed at me. "There she is!" she cried. "That's Randy!"

Ms. Mason was losing her patience. "Don't be shy," she chided me. "Hurry up!"

I slowly climbed down the bleachers and stepped onto the gym floor. Lucas stood off to the side, waiting for me.

We'll have to do swing-your-partner, I realized. I'll have to *touch* him. I'll have to touch a *dead person!*

My stomach rolled over. There was no way I'd square-dance with a dead guy.

"Ms. Mason," I said in a weak voice. "I feel sick."

She frowned. "You do look a little pale."

My stomach churned. I really didn't feel well.

"Maybe you'd better go to the nurse's office," Ms. Mason said.

I hurried out of the gym. I felt Lucas's eyes burning into my back as I left.

"You know, it really wasn't so bad, square dancing," Karla said as we emerged from the Division Street Mall. I'd gone to the movies with her and Kris and Sara. It was eight o'clock and not quite dark yet.

"You might have had fun, Randy," Kris added. "We didn't have to talk to our partners or even touch them that much, except when it was time to swing around."

"If anybody had swung me around, I would have thrown up," I said. "I felt sick just looking at Lucas."

"Get over it," Karla scolded. "Lucas ended up dancing with Marcia Lee, and nothing bad happened to her."

"I think you're getting crazy over this hide-and-seek game," Sara agreed. "I mean, no one's really sure if Pete exists."

I bristled. *"You're* the ones who told me about him! And if it's not true, why do you keep playing this game year after year? Why do kids end up in the insane asylum with their hair all white, never to talk again? It has to be true!"

Kris looked scared. "She's right!"

"Come on, you guys," Sara said. "The game is just for fun! If it's a little scary, that makes it more fun."

"We know lots of kids who have played," Karla insisted. "And nothing bad has ever happened to them."

All right, I thought. So I'm a wimp. But the more I see, the more I believe Pete exists.

We crossed the mall parking lot and started down Division Street. At Park Drive we split up. Sara, Kris, and Karla caught a bus home to North Hills.

I stood on the corner, waiting for my bus. It didn't come.

After about ten minutes I decided to walk home. It was a warm night, and still light out.

It got dark quickly, though. I began to walk faster. I was late and I knew Mom would be worried. I could hear her scolding me already: "I specifically told you to be home before dark."

Too late for that. It was totally dark now.

But I was almost home. I turned the corner onto Fear Street. Up ahead I saw the Fear Street Cemetery.

I couldn't help wishing I *had* made it home before dark. Passing the cemetery is okay in the daytime, but it's not my favorite place to be at night.

67

I hurried past, trying not to think about the voices I'd heard there. Trying not even to look at the place.

But something moved near one of the graves. It caught my eye. I couldn't help it. I had to look.

Something white flashed in the darkness. I moved a little closer. I heard the sound of a spade in the dirt. The sound of digging.

A boy crouched near one of the graves. His face was close to the dirt, as if he were sniffing the ground.

I ducked behind a tree to watch.

It was Lucas!

He pulled something out of the ground and held it up in front of his eyes. It was purple and slimy. And I could see it moving. Wriggling and twisting in Lucas's hand.

A worm.

"Yes!" Lucas cried.

And then he did something that made me sure I'd been right all along.

Lucas slowly lowered the fat purple worm toward his mouth.

I started to scream, but stifled it with my hand. A little squeak still came out.

Lucas jerked his head in my direction.

I ducked into the shadows.

Lucas peered through the darkness. He seemed to be sniffing, trying to catch a scent in the air. I held my breath.

Lucas turned away and started digging again.

As quietly as I could, I slipped across the street. I hid behind a tree and peeked at Lucas. Had he seen me?

He kept on digging, face to the ground.

I hurried down the street, keeping in the shadows. I didn't look back until I was safely inside the house.

I poked my head out the door.

No sign of him. I shut the front door and locked it. I was safe—for now.

Pete controls the body at night, I thought. Now it's nighttime. And Pete has taken poor Lucas out to the cemetery.

I shuddered. June tenth is almost here. What if Pete tags me?

Then *I'll* be out in the cemetery at night. Digging up worms. And eating them. I could almost feel a bunch of wriggling, slimy worms in my stomach.

"Randy, is that you?" Mom called from the den. I took a deep breath and went in. Mom, Dad, and Baby all sat in front of the TV, watching a police show.

"How was the movie?" Dad asked. "Are you hungry? We saved you a little chicken if you want it."

"It's warming in the oven," Mom added.

"I had pizza at the mall," I lied.

I'd actually had nothing but popcorn. But I couldn't imagine eating after what I'd seen Lucas do.

"You're a little late, honey," Mom chided me. "Did you have to wait long for the bus?"

"It didn't come," I told her. "I walked home."

Mom and Dad both turned sharply away from the TV to give me their X-ray glares.

70

Dad's voice was low and serious. "You should have called us, Randy. We would have been glad to pick you up."

"I know. I didn't think it would get dark so soon."

Baby jumped off the couch, blocking everyone's view of the TV.

"Oooo," she squealed. "Randy's going to get in trouble!"

"Be quiet, Baby," I grumped.

"Not Baby, Barbara!" she yelled. "Bar-bar-a!"

"Sit down, Baby," Dad said.

"Barbara!"

"I think it's time for bed, Baby," Mom said. "Come on. Let's go up to bed."

Baby let out an earsplitting scream. *"Barbara!"*

Mom held one hand to her ear. With the other she took Baby by the arm and pulled her upstairs.

"Get the tranquilizer gun," I joked.

Dad frowned at me. "Maybe you should go up to bed, too, young lady. I don't like to think of you walking around alone at night."

"I didn't mean to," I said.

"All right," Dad answered. "Go upstairs anyway, and think about it."

I went up to my room. I put on a summer nightgown and snuggled into bed to read. I had to do something to take my mind off Pete. A warm breeze drifted in through the open window, lightly fluttering the curtains.

I don't remember falling asleep, but I must have. I woke up with a start. My bedside lamp was still on. The book had tumbled to the floor. The rest of the house was quiet. What time is it? I wondered.

I glanced at my alarm clock. One o'clock in the morning.

I pulled down my bedsheets and switched off the light. Across the street all the houses were dark. The street was quiet.

Except for a faint sound.

Voices. Voices coming closer.

"I touched you! You're It!"

"He's coming! He's coming! Run!"

"Ready or not, here I come!"

I sat up, shaking.

The voices came from the woods. "Olly olly oxen free!"

I leaned toward the window and stared out. At first I saw no one. And the voices suddenly stopped.

But then something moved under the light of the street lamp.

A boy. A boy darted out of the shadows. He flashed through the pool of light.

I didn't get a very good look at him. He came from the direction of the woods. Then he disappeared down the street. Toward Lucas's house. It had to be Lucas, I thought. Or Pete. I wasn't sure how to think of him.

But I was scared. He's chosen me, I thought. He's after me.

I'm going to be Pete's next body.

12

"**B**e good, girls." Dad kissed me and Baby on the forehead.

"We won't be back too late," Mom said. "If anything happens, call us at the Lewises'." Sara's parents had invited Mom and Dad over for dinner. "I left their number on the refrigerator."

"And don't forget—Baby goes to bed by eight," Dad added.

"Barbara!" Baby protested. "You keep forgetting!"

Dad was busy looking for his car keys. "Sorry, Baby."

Baby pouted and stamped her foot. Sometimes I feel sorry for her. No one ever listens to her.

But then she'll do something obnoxious—like "accidentally" squirting me with her squirt gun— and I wish she'd get kidnapped by aliens. Preferably aliens whose favorite food is seven-year-old girl.

Baby started whining. "I don't want to go to bed at eight. Why can't I stay up late like Randy?"

"You can stay up late when you're Randy's age," Mom said soothingly. "Just think, that's only five years away!"

Baby burst into tears.

"Five years! That's a long time!"

She ran to her room, wailing.

"Thanks a lot, Mom," I said sarcastically. Mom had upset Baby. But *I* had to go calm her down.

Mom leaned down to kiss me goodbye. "Sorry, honey. She'll quiet down soon."

Dad opened the front door. Mom grabbed her purse.

"Say hi to Sara," I called as they settled into the car.

They drove off, waving.

Baby and I were alone in the house for the evening.

I'd baby-sat for Baby before, of course.

But not on Fear Street. Until tonight.

I dragged myself up to Baby's room. Please don't let her go into full tantrum mode, I prayed. Please let her be good tonight.

Being alone with Baby when she's in full tantrum

mode was my worst nightmare. Even Mom and Dad couldn't handle her then.

Once she threw a quart of milk on the floor. The carton exploded like a bomb. Milk splattered all over the kitchen. Another time she tripped me while I was helping Mom clear the table. I was carrying a stack of dirty plates. They fell facedown on the dining room rug. Mom had to take the rug out to get it cleaned.

"Baby?" I called. "How are you doing?"

I listened for a response. Silence. I didn't hear any crying or whining.

Uh-oh, I thought. Is that good or bad?

"Baby?"

I peered into her bedroom.

She wasn't there.

"Baby! Where are you?"

I stepped into her room, searching for her. I checked under her bed. I checked behind the door.

"Baby?"

What could have happened to her?

I pulled open her dresser drawers—she used to hide in there sometimes when she was smaller. Nothing.

"Baby!" I called again.

Maybe she's in Mom and Dad's room, I thought. I turned to leave.

"Boo!" The closet door flew open. Baby jumped out at me.

I yelled. Baby hopped up and down, laughing.

"I scared you! I scared you! I scared you!"

At least it wasn't a temper tantrum.

"Ha ha, Baby," I fake-laughed. "You scared me. Very funny."

"I scared Randy! I scared Randy!"

"Come on," I said, taking her by her little fist. "Let's eat supper."

After a dinner of microwave pizza and ice cream, Baby and I watched TV. I put her to bed at eight-thirty—I always let her stay up late when I baby-sit—and she fell asleep right away.

I collapsed onto the couch in the den. Whew. That wasn't so bad, I thought, relieved. And it'll be a no-brainer from here on.

I couldn't find anything good on TV. I turned it off and curled up on the couch to read a magazine.

An hour passed. It was almost ten o'clock.

I rolled off the couch and went to the window. Outside the world lay dark and quiet.

I stared out toward the Fear Street Cemetery, listening.

Was Lucas in the cemetery tonight? Was he out there somewhere, digging for food?

I checked the front door to make sure it was locked.

All of a sudden I couldn't relax. The house was too quiet. Things didn't feel right.

I paced from room to room. Living room, dining room, kitchen, den.

Maybe I should turn the TV back on, I thought. It will keep me company.

I switched it on. A police show. "Cops to the Rescue."

I thought I heard a noise. In the hall, outside the den.

I froze, listening. On TV, sirens wailed.

Behind me, something clattered to the floor.

I whirled around.

Baby!

She stared forlornly at the plastic plate she'd dropped. Cookies were scattered across the floor.

"I can't sleep," she whined.

"You have to go to bed," I ordered. "Mom and Dad will be home soon, and if you're still up I'll get in trouble."

"But I'm hungry," she cried. A little sob bubbled up from the back of her throat.

Oh, no, I thought. Tantrum on its way.

I stood up, accidentally crushing a cookie under my shoe. I felt like throwing a tantrum myself.

"Come on, Baby," I said irritably. "Help me pick up these cookies. Then you go back to bed."

"You called me Baby again!" she shouted. "I keep telling you! I want you to call me Barbara!"

I blew it! I tried to hold off the tantrum.

"I'm sorry, I'm sorry," I said, trying to soothe her. "I keep forgetting, Baby."

Oops.

She threw back her head and started screaming. At the top of her lungs.

"WWWAAAAAAAAAAAA!"

"Shush! Shush, Baby!"

"WWWAAAAAAAAAAAAAA!"

I grabbed a cookie off the floor and shoved it toward her face.

"Look!" I shouted over her screams. "Look, Baby. A cookie! Don't you want to eat this yummy cookie?"

"WWWAAAAAAAAAAAAAA!"

I shook her. I petted her. I made funny faces at her. Nothing could make her stop. She screamed her head off.

The neighbors will think I'm killing her, I realized.

Then something changed.

She didn't stop screaming. But her screams sounded different.

They weren't tantrum screams anymore. They were terror screams.

She grabbed me and pointed toward the window.

"AAAAAAAAAAA!"

I turned to look.

Then it was my turn to scream.

13

"**A**aaaaa! Aaaaaa! Help!" I screamed.

Lucas stared at me through the window.

Then he disappeared. And the front door rattled.

He was trying to get into the house!

I raced to the front door and leaned all my weight against it.

The door's locked, I reminded myself. He can't get in.

Then the lock turned.

"No!" I screamed. "Baby, come help me!"

Baby leaned with me. Tears streaked her face.

The door began to open. I pressed against it.

"*No!*" I yelled. "Go away!"

A mighty shove came from the other side of the

door. It flew open, throwing me and Baby out of the way.

"Help!" I shouted. "Stay out! Stay out!"

I hugged Baby, hoping at least to protect her from Lucas.

But Lucas wasn't there.

"Randy! What's the matter?"

I opened my eyes.

Mom and Dad.

I didn't know what to say.

"Randy, are you all right?" Dad demanded.

"I—I—"

"What's going on?" Mom cried.

I felt my cheeks go red and hot.

"Did something happen?" Mom asked. "Was someone trying to get in?"

"Lucas!" I cried. "I saw his face in the window! He's trying to get me!"

Dad frowned. "Who's Lucas?"

"He's Pete!" I replied.

Mom and Dad exchanged baffled looks.

"Isn't Lucas a boy in your class?" Mom asked.

I nodded. I began to realize how crazy I sounded.

Maybe it's better not to tell them, I thought.

What can they do to help me, anyway?

Nothing. They can't do a thing.

"Why would this boy be peeking into our windows?" Dad said. "Maybe I should call the police."

"No—it's okay, Dad," I answered. "I—I probably imagined it."

Mom frowned. "Are you sure, Randy? You seemed awfully frightened."

"I was watching something scary on TV," I lied. "It got to me, that's all."

"I saw him, too!" Baby yelled. "I saw a boy!"

"No, you didn't, Baby," I insisted. "That was on TV."

"It was not!"

"Don't listen to her," I assured Mom and Dad. "You know how she makes things up."

Dad shrugged. "Okay. But if anything else like that happens, let us know."

"I will. I promise."

"I saw him!" Baby cried. "I'm not making it up!"

"Go back to bed, Baby," Mom ordered. "We're all going to bed now."

Dad tried his soothing voice. "That's right, Baby. All us big people are going to bed. Wouldn't you like to be like us?"

"I'm not sleepy!" Baby announced. "I'm wide, wide awake!"

"Well, I guess I'll be going to bed now," I said. "Have fun, you three."

I left Mom and Dad to deal with Baby.

That's it, I thought as I trudged up the stairs.
I've got all the facts I need.
Lucas is Pete.
And Pete will do anything to get me.
Even try to break into my house.
I'm doomed.

14

Crash!

The glass slipped from my hand and smashed on the kitchen floor. Orange juice trickled over the tiles and settled in a crack by the cabinets.

"Rats!" I muttered. I grabbed some paper towels and swabbed at the juice.

"Be careful of the glass, Randy." Mom watched me, frowning. "Are you feeling all right, honey?"

"Sure, sure." I tried to hide my face from her so she wouldn't see how nervous I felt.

Saturday, the tenth of June had arrived.

I'd woken up that morning with a small, hard knot in the pit of my stomach.

The knot grew bigger as the day went on. I tried

to read. I tried to watch cartoons with Baby, but I couldn't sit still. I paced through the house like a caged animal.

"Randy, you're making me nervous," Mom said that afternoon. "Why don't you run out to the store for me? I need a pound of ground beef."

Run out to the store? Did she actually want me to go outside?

"I can't, Mom."

"Why not? It's a perfectly lovely day. You could use some fresh air."

"I really don't feel like it—"

She plunked some money into my palm and pushed me out the door. "Go!" she ordered. "One pound of lean ground beef. Thank you."

The streets seemed oddly quiet for a Saturday afternoon. Usually the neighborhood is full of kids out playing or whizzing around on their bikes.

Not that day. There wasn't much traffic. I saw one man mowing his lawn.

But mostly, I had the feeling people were holed up inside their houses—especially the kids. I imagined them sitting nervously at home, storing up their energy.

They'd need it for the game that night. No one wanted to be tagged by Pete.

No one wanted to be It next year.

* * *

Sara called during dinner that evening.

She almost whispered into the phone. "Don't forget. The game begins just after dark."

"How could I forget? It's all I've been able to think about for weeks."

"Listen, Randy," Sara went on. "Suppose your crazy idea is right. Suppose Lucas really is Pete. All you have to do is stay away from him. He won't be able to tag you, now that you know. . . ."

She's right, I thought. I'll just stay away from him, and I'll be fine.

"I'll meet you there," I said.

"Great." Sara sounded relieved. "See you tonight."

I returned to the table. Baby wolfed down her meat loaf. I wasn't very hungry. But I tried to swallow a few bites of potato. I needed my strength.

I could feel Mom watching me in that worried way out of the corner of her eye. Dad ate cheerfully.

"Big night tonight, huh?" he said to me. "Looking forward to it, Randy?"

I kept my eyes on my plate. "Uh-huh."

"A good game of hide-and-seek. Sounds like fun to me. You'll be part of an old Shadyside tradition."

"Yeah."

"After tonight you'll feel like a true citizen of the town," he went on. "You'll bond with the other kids. It's like an initiation or something."

Clearly Dad didn't know what he was talking about. I wished he'd be quiet.

Mom spoke up. "It's not dangerous or anything, is it, Randy?"

"No," I answered in a small voice. I hate lying to my mother. "How could it be dangerous? It's a simple game of hide-and-seek."

"Relax, honey," Dad said. "I'm sure there's nothing to worry about."

"I want to play hide-and-seek," Baby demanded.

"When you're older, Baby," Dad told her. "Your turn will come."

"I want to play now!"

"Behave yourself, Baby," Mom warned. "You want to get sent to bed early?"

"My name is Barbara!"

I set down my fork and watched Baby from across the table. It was weird to think that in a few years she'd be in my place.

She gets on my nerves. But I'd hate to see her controlled by a ghost. She doesn't bother me *that* much.

I pushed my chair away from the table. "May I be excused?"

"You've hardly touched your dinner," Mom noted.

I speared a bite of meat loaf and popped it into my mouth. Just to make her happy.

"I'm full," I replied, chewing. "I'm going upstairs to lie down for a while."

As I left the kitchen I heard Dad saying to Mom, "I'm sure it's nothing, honey. She's probably nervous because she doesn't know too many other kids. Don't forget, she's the new girl at school."

That's right, I thought as I trudged up the steps. I'm the new girl.

And Pete likes new kids.

We all gathered on the edge of the Fear Street Woods.

This part of Fear Street had no streetlights. Clouds shifted over the half-moon. Some kids carried flashlights. From a distance the lights looked like giant eyes.

My heart raced. I wandered through the crowd of kids my age, hoping to find Sara or Kris and Karla. I peered into people's faces, searching for someone I knew. They stared back at me. Our eyes would meet for a second, then dart away.

I think everyone felt as nervous as I did. No one said much.

Then I saw someone I knew.

Lucas.

He started toward me.

Stay away from me! I silently screamed.

I can't let him near me.

I dodged away. I tried to lose myself in the crowd.

I didn't know where I would hide. But it didn't matter. As long as I avoided Lucas.

Mr. Sirk, the boys' gym teacher, stood off to the side. He watched us, his face strangely grim. I wondered why he was there.

Slowly, silently, more kids arrived. We hovered around, expectantly. Everyone kept an eye on Mr. Sirk, as if waiting for some kind of signal from him.

At last he waved his flashlight. We crowded around him.

Mr. Sirk spoke in a low, solemn voice I'd never heard him use before.

"Welcome, kids. As you know, tonight is the tenth of June—Pete's birthday.

"You are here to participate in an old Shadyside ritual: a game of hide-and-seek.

"Generations of Shadyside kids have played. You are following in the footsteps of your parents and grandparents. After tonight none of you will be the same."

Mr. Sirk gave a creepy mad-scientist laugh. A couple kids snickered, but most didn't even smile.

We listened to every word he said, more quietly and more obediently than we ever did at school.

"For the majority of you, the game will be just that—a game," Mr. Sirk went on. "But for one of you, there is a great deal at stake. I think you all know what I mean."

My stomach flipped. Not me. Don't let it be me.

"The rules are simple: No flashlights allowed. You'll leave your flashlights here by the road.

"At the signal you'll run into the woods to hide."

We all turned our eyes to the woods. They stood deep, dark, and silent, ready to swallow us.

He patted a huge, gnarled old tree. "This is home base. If you touch it on your way out of the woods, you're safe. But you must stay in the woods and hide for at least half an hour. No one is safe before half an hour passes."

He paused. None of us moved. We waited to hear more. My heartbeat throbbed in my ears.

At last Mr. Sirk spoke again. "I guess you all know who's It."

No one said a word. We all knew.

It was Pete's birthday. Pete was It.

Mr. Sirk cleared his throat. "Good luck to you all. And please be very careful."

Someone struck a match. In the glow I saw Sara's face. She lit twelve candles. Twelve candles on top of a big birthday cake.

Two girls I didn't know helped Sara lift up the cake. The candlelight threw weird shadows on their faces.

Across the top of the cake, scrawled in red frosting, I saw the words "Happy Birthday Pete."

Everyone began to sing.

"Happy birthday to you."

I'd never heard "Happy Birthday" sung so grimly. But then, I'd never been to a birthday party for a ghost before.

I joined in. We sang very slowly.

We're all secretly trying to put this off, I thought. To put off playing this game for as long as we can.

The song ended. Everyone stood still as statues, waiting.

Waiting for what? I wondered.

What is the signal?

I saw Sara's mouth twitch nervously in the candlelight.

Suddenly the candles went out.

Only I didn't see anyone blow on them.

The woods were pitch black.

The game had begun.

15

Everybody ran.

Sara and the other girls dropped the cake. *Splat!* It smashed in the dirt. Kids trampled it as they raced into the woods.

We all spread out. Sara glanced back and saw me. She beckoned me to follow her.

I shook my head. Pete would find two of us more easily than one.

I stopped a few yards into the woods. Which way to go?

I heard footsteps behind me and turned. A boy ran straight for me.

Lucas!

No. Another boy. He brushed past me and disappeared behind a tree.

No sign of Lucas. Safe for now.

I scurried along a narrow path, deeper into the woods. Kids ran everywhere. I heard shrieks and laughter and screams all around me.

No one had found a place to hide yet. I had to get away from them. I had to go deeper into the woods.

I peered through the darkness as I ran. My feet crunched on the low shrubs. My thoughts raced.

Quiet! I scolded myself. You've got to be silent!

Where can I hide?

These woods are huge, I realized. I felt lost in them.

All the other kids seemed to have disappeared. I kind of wished I'd see someone I knew. Sara or Kris or somebody. Anybody but Lucas.

I pushed on into the woods. I'm all alone, I thought.

No. I'm not alone.

Crunch crunch crunch.

I tried to listen. My heartbeat pounded in my head. I stood still.

Twigs crackled. Footsteps behind me.

I glanced back. Who's there? I didn't see anyone. But I heard someone.

Crunch crunch crunch.

Getting closer.

Maybe it's Sara, I wished. Or some other friend. But the longer I stood still the more scared I felt.

I took a deep breath. I can't wait to find out who this is, I realized. I have to get away!

I started to run again. I ran faster.

Crunch crunch crunch.

Closer. Closer.

I swerved off the path, hoping the footsteps wouldn't follow. I crashed through bushes and low branches.

Crunch crunch crunch.

Headed right for me. Still closer.

Someone was chasing me!

16

I whirled around.

Lucas?

No.

No one.

The footsteps had stopped. There was no one behind me.

Forget it, I told myself. Keep running.

I plunged blindly through the woods. I dodged the trees in my way. Branches snapped in my face, stinging my eyes.

I came to another path. I paused.

Crunch crunch crunch.

There they were again. The footsteps!

I spun around.

The crunching sounds stopped.

I strained my eyes, staring through the darkness. No one there.

I wish I had a flashlight, I thought. Why aren't we allowed to have flashlights?

No time to worry about it. I turned onto the new path and raced on.

I stumbled over rocks and roots, panting. I can't run much farther, I realized.

I've got to rest.

The footsteps kept getting closer, closer.

They'll catch up to me soon.

I've got to hide. But where?

Nothing around but trees. Got to hide in a tree.

I grabbed the nearest branch and pulled myself up.

I climbed as high as I could. The bark scraped my hands. I settled in a crook of the tree, catching my breath.

I stared down. I should have picked a taller tree, I thought. Maybe then I could spot Lucas coming.

Now I can't see anything but leaves.

At least they'll hide me well.

Pete won't find me. He'll never see me up here.

I sat for several minutes, perfectly still.

Not a sound in the woods.

What happened to those footsteps? I wondered.

And how much time has gone by? Ten minutes? Fifteen?

How will I know when half an hour has passed?

I wish I had a glow-in-the-dark watch.

No. Pete would see it for sure.

I clung to the branch, waiting.

The tree began to shake.

I froze.

Stay calm, I told myself.

It's the wind. It must be the wind.

I hadn't heard any footsteps. I hadn't heard anyone approach.

So it has to be the wind. Right?

The tree shook harder. Too hard. And I didn't feel any breeze.

It wasn't the wind.

My mind raced. Stay here! Stay here!

I'm safe here. I *must* be!

But all at once I knew I wasn't safe.

I knew it. I felt it.

Hot breath on my neck.

Someone was in the tree with me.

Right next to me.

So close he could touch me.

17

I was afraid to look. But I had to.

I twisted my head around.

A boy! A boy sat beside me in the darkness.

Not Lucas.

David.

Blond David in a white T-shirt. It was easy to see his pale hair and pale shirt in the faint moonlight.

I started to breathe again.

What a relief. It was only David.

"Hi," he whispered. He shifted, and the branch shook.

"Shhh!" I hissed. "Careful! You're making too much noise."

I was glad to have him there, though.

Maybe I was wrong to try to hide alone, I thought. It's too scary.

It felt better to have company.

"Don't worry, Randy," David said. "Pete won't get you as long as you're with me."

I smiled. David's nice, I thought. He's really the best person who could have turned up.

He spied on Lucas with me. He understands how scary it is.

"I'm glad you're here, David," I whispered. "We'll be safe now."

He nodded. "Everything's going to be fine."

We sat in silence for a long time, waiting.

"Maybe we can make a break for it soon," I murmured. "We can run for home base together."

"Soon," David answered. "Not yet."

The woods were completely silent. I felt good. It was almost over.

Then I noticed a funny smell.

The faint odor of garbage.

I sniffed.

Or maybe rotten vegetables?

Where was it coming from?

The smell grew stronger.

"Do you smell something?" I asked. "It's gross."

David shook his head. "I don't smell anything."

"Funny," I said. The odor grew worse by the second. I began to feel a little sick to my stomach.

"It's as if we're hiding in a garbage truck," I said. "Worse, even."

David shrugged.

And then I realized—the smell came from David.

David smelled funny.

David smelled *horrible*.

At first I felt embarrassed.

I shouldn't have said anything, I thought.

Maybe he forgot to take a bath or something.

But the smell kept getting stronger.

Worse than someone who never takes a bath.

Worse than fifty garbage trucks.

I choked. I wanted to hold my nose. But that would have been rude.

I studied David more closely.

His white shirt had a stain on it. A dark stain the size of a quarter, right on his chest. I didn't think much of it.

But when I looked at him again, the stain had grown. Now it was as big as a CD.

He smelled bad and his shirt was stained. I never knew David was such a slob.

I pointed to the stain.

"What happened?" I asked. "Did you spill something?"

101

"In a way," he answered.

Strange. Now his voice sounded funny, too.

Not quite right. Not like David's usual voice. A bit higher.

Without thinking, I slid away from him a little.

"This game's so stupid," David said. His voice changed more.

"Pete's not so bad. I don't know why everybody tries so hard to get away."

The voice had completely transformed now. Not David's voice at all.

I sat frozen in the tree, staring at him. The stain spread across his shirt, slowly growing bigger.

"What is everybody so afraid of?" the boy beside me demanded. "Pete always gives the bodies back.

"I give them back as good as new."

Alarms shrieked in my head.

I.

He said *I!*

The boy smiled at me. He didn't look like David anymore.

His teeth were crooked, rotten and black.

His breath blasted me in the face, hot and stinking.

And the stain on his shirt began to drip.

Drip, drip.

102

A drop fell onto my hand. I held my hand up to my eyes and stared at the drop.

Dark red. Warm.

Blood.

He was Pete!

18

"**D**on't worry, Randy," Pete croaked. A decayed tooth fell out of his mouth as he spoke.

"It won't hurt a bit. It's not so bad to let me take over your body.

"Think about it—you'll never be lonely."

I didn't wait around to hear more. I scrambled out of that tree as fast as I could.

The bark scraped my hands, but I didn't care.

"Don't run," Pete called after me. "I'll catch you. You can't get away from me."

I jumped out of the tree. I fell ten feet, landing on the soft dirt below.

Then I sprang up and raced for home base.

I didn't look back.

I didn't have to. I could feel Pete's hot, stinky breath on the back of my neck.

I stumbled through the woods. Branches clawed at me. I slapped them away.

Pete's heavy footsteps pounded behind me.

I had no time to think about which way to go. I ran.

I hoped I was headed for the edge of the woods.

I had to get to home base. If I could tag that oak tree, I'd be safe.

I heard Pete's voice, almost in my ear.

"It's hopeless, Randy," he called. He wasn't panting or out of breath. I guess ghosts don't get tired.

But I knew I couldn't run much longer.

Where was that stupid oak tree?

Then I heard voices.

Kids' voices.

I swerved toward them.

I saw it.

The edge of the woods. Home base.

Kids stood by the oak tree, waving flashlights.

"Hurry!" they called. "You're almost home!"

"You won't make it!" Pete's voice cried. "Give up now, Randy. You can't beat me!"

No! No, no, no!

I won't give up. I won't.

I'm going to make it home.

The tree stood only a few yards away. I held my arms out in front of me, reaching, reaching . . .

Something caught my foot.

I stumbled and lost my balance.

I fell flat on my face.

I was trapped.

19

~~~

"**N**o!" I screamed.

He's got me. He's going to take my body. Would it hurt?

I scrambled to my feet. Pete reached out to tag me, his fingers less than an inch from my arm.

"Hey, Pete!" a familiar voice called. "What are you going to do? Spend a whole year in a *girl's* body?"

Pete hesitated. He turned and peered into the woods.

Lucas appeared between two trees, dancing around like a boxer. He laughed. "A girl named Pete—that's a good one! We'll have fun all year teasing you about that!"

Pete stared at him, growling like an animal.

"Come and get me, Pete!" Lucas taunted. "Or should I say 'Petina'!"

Lucas disappeared behind the trees. "Do you have to pick on a girl, Pete?" he yelled. "Afraid you can't catch a guy?"

Pete tore after him.

"Go, Lucas!" I screamed. "You can do it!"

A boy in a green T-shirt cut in front of Pete. Charging toward home base.

Pete turned and lunged toward the boy. He missed. He spun around and headed back in the direction we had seen Lucas.

I realized I hadn't tagged home. I threw myself at home base. I didn't just touch the tree—I hugged it.

I was safe. Safe forever. Or at least for a whole year.

But what about Lucas? I stared around the woods, searching for him. I heard someone crashing through the bushes. Did Pete catch Lucas? Or had Lucas found a new place to hide?

I can't believe how wrong I was, I thought, panting.

Lucas wasn't Pete. It was David all along. And I asked him to help me spy on Lucas!

Kids still darted through the woods. I clutched the tree, safe, listening to their shouts.

Who was Pete chasing now?

Sara suddenly appeared, dashing for home. She slammed against the tree.

"You made it!" I cried, hugging her. "We're safe!"

She nodded, catching her breath. We hung around, waiting for other kids to come in.

Megan appeared, and then Karla and Kris. I watched for Lucas, but I didn't see him.

A good sign, I thought. The longer he's out, the more likely it is he got away from Pete.

"That was fun!" Kris exclaimed. "It wasn't scary at all."

"Sure," Karla joked. "You weren't scared. You only screamed every time I touched you."

"Well, you could have been Pete!" Kris protested.

"Pete almost got me," I told them. "But Lucas saved me!"

"Lucas?" Sara sounded confused. "But you said he was Pete."

"He wasn't," I explained. *"David* was!"

"No way," Megan shot back. "You're making that up, Randy."

"I am not! David was Pete! He chased me, but Lucas saved me just in time!"

"I'm sure David was just having fun with you," Megan insisted. "He's *not* Pete."

"He is!" Why wouldn't they believe me?

"Okay, Randy. We believe you." Sara rolled her eyes, and the other girls giggled.

109

"Ask David," I demanded. "He'll tell you."

We glanced around, but there was no sign of David.

"You'll call him tonight and get him to go along with your story," Megan said.

"You'll see," I told them. "Monday morning David will come into school with gray hair or something. Then you'll believe me."

"I'll believe you got him to dye his hair somehow, that's what I'll believe," Karla teased.

More kids sprinted out of the woods and tagged the tree. They milled around with their flashlights, talking and laughing.

Mr. Sirk blew a whistle. "Game over!" he announced. "Until this time next year."

Everyone clapped and cheered. We were all so happy the game was over. Kids started to wander away in groups of twos and threes.

"Has anyone seen Lucas?" I asked.

"I saw Lucas as I was running for home," Kris answered.

"Was he all right?" I asked her.

Kris shrugged. "He looked fine to me."

"He probably tagged home while we were talking and then left," Sara suggested.

Good, I thought. Lucas is okay. Maybe Pete couldn't catch anyone this year.

I've got to apologize to Lucas, I decided. And thank him.

And explain why I avoided him all this time.

More kids headed out of the woods. People waved their flashlights. "See you next year, Pete!"

I said goodbye to Sara and Kris and Karla. I walked home alone. It had been a terrifying night. But it's over now! I thought.

Even alone in the dark I don't feel afraid. I don't feel afraid of anything anymore! I felt so happy.

No more Pete!

On Monday morning I strolled through the crowded halls, keeping an eye out for Lucas. I didn't find him, so I went to class.

"I hope you and David got your stories straight," Megan teased.

"He'll back me up," I insisted. "You'll see."

But David never showed up. The first bell rang and Ms. Hartman closed the door. David's seat was empty.

Where was he?

A boy whispered something to Megan. She passed it along to me.

"Somebody heard David had to go to the hospital," she whispered. "Do you think—?"

I nodded. Poor David.

* * *

111

Sara and I passed the baseball field after school that day. Shadyside was playing Hartsdale. I hadn't seen Lucas all day. I couldn't wait to talk to him.

We settled in the bleachers to watch. Lucas stood on the pitcher's mound. He whizzed the ball past the Hartsdale batter.

"Kris said she heard David's okay," Sara told me. "He's supposed to get out of the hospital tomorrow."

"What's wrong with him?" I asked.

"I don't know. Some kind of virus or something . . ."

"I'm telling you he was Pete! That's what made him sick."

"Okay, okay."

"Strike three!" Lucas struck out the first batter. Sara and I clapped.

"What are you going to say to Lucas?" Sara asked as we watched the game.

"I'm not sure," I replied. "I guess I'll explain that it was a misunderstanding. It sounds kind of silly now."

Shadyside beat Hartsdale five to three. I hung around, waiting for Lucas to come off the field.

Sara nudged me. "I guess you want to thank him by yourself. Call me and let me know what happens."

"Okay," I agreed.

She gave me a playful little wave and dashed off.

Lucas ambled off the field. He carried his bat over one shoulder. His baseball mitt hung off the end of it.

"Hi," I said.

"Hi," he said back. He smiled. "That was some game of hide-and-seek the other night, wasn't it?"

"Yeah," I agreed.

We began to walk toward home.

"Are you all right?" he asked. "You didn't get hurt or anything, did you?"

"I'm fine," I answered. "How about you? Are you okay?"

"Great." He grinned.

He took off his baseball cap and pushed a lock of curly dark hair off his forehead.

He's really cute, I thought. Why didn't I notice that before?

I took a deep breath. Apology time.

"Lucas—I can't believe what you did for me. Pete would have gotten me for sure if it weren't for you."

"No big deal." He put his cap back on, shrugging.

"It's a big deal to me. Especially since—well, I guess I haven't been very nice to you."

"You kept running away from me," he said. "I did kind of notice that."

113

"Well, you know, I can explain," I stammered. "See, I thought—"

I paused.

"It seems so stupid now I'm embarrassed to say it."

We crossed the street. He looked at me, waiting to hear what I had to say. His expression was so friendly I decided to go for it.

"Um, I thought you were Pete."

Lucas laughed. "You thought *I* was Pete? Why?"

This part was embarrassing, too. Should I admit that David and I had spied on him?

No, I decided. I may like to *get* all the facts, but that doesn't mean I like to *give* them all.

"Well," I began, "one night I happened to be passing by, and I saw you in the cemetery. You were digging worms, and I thought Pete was looking for food."

Now Lucas laughed really hard.

"So," I went on, "what were you doing?"

"I was digging worms. You know, night crawlers? But not to eat. To use for fishing bait."

"Oh." I laughed with relief. "Fishing. Why didn't I think of that?"

Then I remembered another strange thing.

"Can I ask you something else?" I began. "Did you come to my house one night and look through the window? I was sure I saw you—"

He laughed again. "I did. I was passing your house on my way home from digging night crawlers, and I heard this terrible screaming—"

Screaming? Oh, yes. Of course.

Baby.

"And I thought maybe you were in trouble. I saw a light on and ran to the window to make sure you were all right."

"Then my parents came home," I finished for him. "And what happened to you?"

"I felt weird about peeking through your windows, so I ran away."

We turned onto Fear Street, both laughing. The sky instantly darkened. I'd noticed that happened a lot on Fear Street.

I paused for breath. Lucas kept laughing.

He laughed harder and harder. His laughter began to sound weird to me.

Not so jolly and happy. More raspy and harsh, as if he had a cold or something.

I glanced at him. His face looked strange. Distorted.

His mouth twisted into a crooked grin. Or was it a scowl?

The trees are throwing shadows on us, I thought. That's why he looks creepy.

He squinted at me, his eyes glittering.

"You know," he rasped, "Pete really wanted you."

115

My heart began to pound.

There is no reason to be afraid of Lucas now, I ordered myself.

"You got away from him." Lucas's voice sounded angry. "That wasn't supposed to happen."

"What?" I didn't understand.

Then I smelled something bad. Rotten.

That same rotten odor I smelled in the woods.

I stared at Lucas. His face twisted horribly now. His mouth pulled into a tortured grimace. His eyes bulged and crossed. The skin on his cheeks tightened over the bones.

He opened his grotesque mouth to speak. His rotten breath blasted into my face.

"It wasn't fair!" he yelled. "I really wanted you!"

He grabbed me.

"No!" I screamed.

Pete!

20

His hand gripped my arm, his fingers digging into my skin. I didn't care. I ripped my arm away and ran.

"You can't get away from me!" he shouted. "I'm going to get you! I don't want Lucas—I want you!"

No way! I thought. But I didn't waste any breath yelling it. I turned in the direction of home and ran.

I had to take the shortest way. I didn't care if I had to run through other people's yards, or through the woods, or—

The cemetery. The Fear Street Cemetery.

I was headed straight for it.

I can't turn away now, I thought. It's the fastest route home.

I glanced back. Pete was speeding toward me. If I paused for one second—*bam!*—he'd catch me!

I didn't hesitate. I raced through the cemetery gates.

Stay calm, I told myself. Just cross through the cemetery. Then you'll be safe.

Behind me Pete's footsteps echoed closer and closer.

"Give up, Randy!" he yelled. His stinky breath washed over me. "Pete likes new kids. . . ."

I pumped my legs harder. I nearly tripped over a headstone. I dodged it. I jumped over another one. I trampled over the graves, crushing old dead flowers underfoot.

Then a hand reached up—up out of a grave— and grabbed my ankle.

21

I wrenched my ankle free. I glanced back.

There was no ghostly hand. Just a vine of ivy straggling across the path.

And pounding closer, Pete's heavy steps.

I jumped to my feet and started running again.

Don't worry about the graveyard, I scolded myself. Don't worry about ghosts. There are no ghosts.

Except Pete.

And that see-through girl standing in front of me. What!

See-through girl?

She opened her mouth and blasted me with icy breath.

"Home base is the other way!" she shrieked.

I stopped dead.

A ghost girl!

I started to turn around. But the other way led to Pete.

Trapped!

And then I heard them.

The sounds that had been haunting me at night. "Olly olly oxen free!"

Childish voices shrieked all around me. "Ready or not, here I come!"

One by one they rose from their graves. Ghost children. Pale, white, nearly transparent. Girls and boys of all ages. All dead. All ghosts, icy cold.

"You're It!" they screeched. "You're It!"

They crowded around me, howling and moaning. Their ashen faces were small and sweet, but twisted with anger. They wore old, tattered clothes—long dresses with torn skirts and schoolboy knickers rotting apart.

What are they going to do to me?

The screaming grew louder, their breath icier.

I shivered in the sudden chill. I scanned the cemetery, searching for a way to escape.

They pressed in, closer, closer.

Anyone around our base is dead, they shrieked.

I covered my ears against their shrill voices.

I spun around. Pete leaned against a tree, watching me. I was trapped!

One of the ghost boys noticed Pete. "You loser!"

the ghost boy yelled. "Not good enough to play with us, right, Pete? Stupid humans are the only ones you can beat!"

The ghost children danced by me, taunting me. "You can't get away now! Oh, no, you can't get away!"

"Try to escape," a dead girl whispered. "I dare you!"

"Help!" I screamed. "Help!"

But the ghost voices grew louder and shriller, covering my screams with their own.

"Five, ten, fifteen, twenty . . ."

No one would hear me.

No one would save me.

Pete was ready to pounce on me if I ran.

The ghosts moved closer and closer.

They closed in on three sides of me. Pete waited behind me.

"Forty-five, fifty, fifty-five . . ."

They're counting to a hundred, I realized.

And then what will they do?

What happens when they get to one hundred?

"Ninety, ninety-five—

"One hundred!"

That's it, I thought.

It's all over.

No, I ordered myself. Don't give up.

"Hey!" I yelled as the ghosts flew at me. "I thought only loser ghosts played with humans. You are no better than Pete."

"Pete's a loser!" a ghost boy shouted.

"Loser! Loser!" the others taunted.

"Yeah. Pete is a loser!" I yelled. "He couldn't even catch me—a human—in the hide-and-seek game last night!"

Pete howled in fury.

"You cheated!" he shrieked. "But I'm still going to win!"

Pete lunged at me, but the boy ghost slid between us, chanting,

> "Pete, Pete,
> Smell my feet.
> Give me something
> Good to eat!"

More ghosts circled around Pete.

"Stop playing with stupid humans, Pete," a girl chided.

"Yeah, Pete!" screeched another ghost. "You're such a loser."

"What's the matter? You afraid of us, Pete?"

"You don't seem so scary now, Pete," I taunted. "You're afraid to leave that human body, aren't you?"

I could see Pete. The ghosts whipped around him. Pete's face popped out through Lucas's. His mouth twisted with anger. His eyes bulged.

One of the ghost children tweaked his nose, and Pete jerked his head back inside Lucas's body.

"Pete, your mom says get out of that body and back into your grave—right this minute!" the ghost girl teased.

"Are you too scared to play with us, Pete?" they shouted. "You have to pick on stupid human kids?"

Most of the ghosts stopped paying attention to me. They circled faster and faster around Pete. Slowly I began to inch away.

A ghost girl shouted, "Hey, Pete—catch!" She plucked off her head, bonnet and all, and tossed it at Pete. He caught it and stared at it, horrified. The disembodied head giggled and flew back on top of the girl's neck.

I forced myself not to scream. I didn't want the ghosts to turn on me.

A boy stuck his face in Pete's and blew out his icy breath. Pete shivered. A little beard of icicles formed on his chin.

"You're It, Pete!" they chanted. "You're It, you're It, you're It!"

Lucas's body began to shake. It quivered, faster and faster.

What's happening?

For a few seconds I saw two bodies—Lucas's and another boy's. Pete's smelly, rotten-toothed body. Messy hair, freckles, dressed in ragged old clothes. But clear and filmy, like the ghosts'.

Then Pete pulled himself back into Lucas.

"I won't come out!" Pete cried.

If I ran now, I could get away.

No, I thought. I have to save Lucas.

"I knew you were afraid, Pete!" I screamed. "You are afraid of the other ghosts. You are even afraid to come after me unless you are safe in someone else's body!"

"Yeah!" the ghost children shouted.

"If you won't come out yourself, we'll suck you out!" a ghost child declared.

The ghosts spun around Lucas and Pete. I watched them whirl around like a cold, white tornado.

"No!" Pete cried. "I want to stay with the humans!"

The spinning ghosts laughed.

"They're too easy to beat!" one shouted.

"Don't be a wimp. Play with us!"

Pete's freckly face rose out of Lucas's head. Then his neck was sucked out, and his torso and legs. With a loud *thwock!* the white whirlpool yanked Pete's body away and up into the air.

He struggled as he spun around like laundry in the rinse cycle.

They sucked him away, back into the cemetery.

They sucked him down, down into a grave.

A grave marked PETER JONES.

"I want to play with Randy!" he protested. Then his head was sucked below the ground.

Laughing, the other ghosts returned to their graves. I thought I heard one of them say, "Pete's a spoiled brat. He wants to be It all the time!"

22

The icy wind died. Lucas and I found ourselves standing alone in the silent graveyard.

No sign of the ghosts. No sign of Pete.

It was as if nothing had happened. Except to Lucas.

I stared at him. His face had turned pale, almost green.

But was he really Lucas again? Or still Pete?

I sniffed him warily. No bad smell. He was his old Lucas self again.

"Are you okay?" I asked.

He patted his hair, trying to make it go back to normal.

"I'm okay, I guess," he replied. "Whew. Thanks for saving me from Pete."

"I owed you one," I told him. I scanned the graveyard once more. All the ghosts were gone. And Pete, too.

"Let's get out of here," I suggested.

Lucas took my hand. We walked out of the cemetery on shaky legs.

"You know," he said, "hide-and-seek is a real baby game."

"Yeah," I agreed. "We're way too old for it."

"We sure are," Lucas declared. "I'm never playing hide-and-seek again."

"Me, neither."

And I never did.

WHO'S BEEN SLEEPING IN MY GRAVE?

Believe me, it isn't easy walking to school with your nose stuck in a book. In two blocks I had already tripped over a curb and bumped into a mailbox.

But I had to finish *Power Kids!*

"The sooner you read it, the sooner you'll be free from terror forever," the cover claimed. And if you know Shadyside, you know why I *needed* to finish the book—fast.

In regular towns you worry about regular things.

In Shadyside you worry about ghosts.

At least I do.

I'm scared of the ghost who wants to play hide-and-seek with kids in the Fear Street woods. I've never seen it myself. But I know people who have.

I'm scared of the burned-out Fear Street mansion. Ghosts have lived there for years and years. At least that's what my friends in school tell me.

And I have nightmares about Fear Street. It's the creepiest street in town—maybe in the whole world. Kevin, my fifteen-year-old brother, says the ghosts that haunt Fear Street are really evil. And horrible things will happen if they catch you.

I think Kevin is really evil. He loves trying to scare me.

But he won't be able to—not after I finish *Power Kids!* Nothing will scare me then. The book guarantees it—or I get my money back.

The kids in my class are going to be pretty upset. They love scaring me, too. Especially on Halloween—which is this Friday, only five days away.

Last Halloween they convinced me that a ghost salesman ran the shoe section in Dalby's Department Store. So I wore high-tops with huge holes in them all winter long. My toes froze.

Sometimes I imagine my friends keeping score. Whoever comes up with the story that scares me the most wins.

I hate it! But I'm almost a Power Kid now. So they'll have to find a new game this Halloween.

"Hey, Zack!" someone yelled.

I didn't bother to glance up from my book. It was Chris Hassler—one of my friends from school.

Chris and I are really different. Chris is short and chubby. He has bright red, curly hair and lots of freckles. Chris is usually laughing—or seems as if he's about to.

I do not look as if I'm about to burst out laughing. Big surprise, right? My grandmother says I have "very serious" eyes, like all the men in the Pepper family.

I have straight brown hair and I'm much taller than Chris. In fact, I'm the tallest kid in the fifth grade.

"Hey, Zack, wait up!" Chris called.

I kept my eyes glued to *Power Kids!* and walked faster.

Chris grabbed my arm as I hurried by his front gate. "Didn't you hear me?" he asked.

"Of course I heard you." I jerked my arm away. "I was trying to ignore you."

I crammed *Power Kids!* into my book bag as fast as I could. Chris would laugh his guts out if he spotted it.

3

"What are you hiding in there?" Chris demanded.

"Something my grandmother gave me for my birthday last week," I said.

"Your grandmother didn't give you any book! She gave you those polka-dot socks. I was at your party. Remember?"

"How could I forget?"

Chris grinned. "Come on. The snake I gave you was a cool present. I can't help it if you thought it was real. And you screamed your head off."

I reached into my backpack and pulled out the slimy rubber snake. "Well, it could have been real!" I shook it in his face.

Chris slapped the snake away. "If you hate it so much, how come you're carrying it around?"

"So I never forget how everyone laughed when I threw the box across the room," I explained. "Every time I see that snake, it will remind me not to let anyone scare me. Ever. Especially you." I returned the rubber snake to my backpack.

"Aw, come on, Zack," Chris whined. "Can't you take one little joke?"

"It's not one little joke," I insisted. "It's a lot of big jokes. Only they're not funny. They're mean!"

"It's not like I *tried* to be mean." Chris sounded hurt.

4

"Yeah, right." I snorted. "You thought I *wanted* to make a fool of myself at my own party."

"I'm sorry, Zack," he said quietly. "You're my best friend. And I really need to talk to you about something. Something serious."

"What?" I asked.

Chris slowly walked back toward his front door, his head down. He sat on the steps. I followed him.

"It's about a dog," Chris began. He talked so low I could hardly hear him. "I'm really worried about it."

"You're worried about a dog?" I said.

Chris peered left, then right. To see if anyone was listening. Then he whispered, "This isn't a regular dog. It's a ghost dog."

"A ghost dog!" I glared at Chris. "I know what you're trying to—"

"I'm not kidding this time," Chris interrupted. "I'm not. And I'm really scared."

Remember the snake, Zack, I told myself. Remember the snake. But then I noticed Chris's hands. They were trembling. Now I felt bad for being suspicious. "Okay," I said. "Tell me about it."

"Well, about a week ago we started hearing a dog howling in the middle of the night. We searched for it. But we never found it. Then last night, my dad . . ." Chris hesitated.

"What?" I demanded.

"Last night my dad was taking the garbage out. And the ghost dog lunged for him." Chris swallowed hard.

"Why do you think it's a *ghost* dog?" I asked.

Chris inhaled deeply. "Dad used the garbage can lid to shield himself—but the dog jumped right through it.

Now my hands began to tremble.

"Wh-what does the ghost dog look like?" I stammered.

"It's pure white, with a big black spot on one side," Chris replied.

"Dad's sure the dog will be back tonight. And I'm really afraid."

Chris had barely finished his sentence when we heard it.

Howling.

I jerked my head up—and there it was. Coming right at me. A white dog. With a big black spot on its side.

The ghost dog!

2

The ghost dog growled. A mean growl. Then he leaped on top of me and knocked me down. The back of my head hit the top step with a thud.

A drop of the dog's hot saliva dripped down my neck.

I squeezed my eyes shut. I'm dead meat. Dead meat.

"Here, boy!" Chris yelled.

My eyes shot wide open. Chris stood over me, hugging the ghost dog.

"Gotcha!" he cried. "This is my cousin's dog. We're keeping him while my cousin's on vacation!"

I jumped up and grabbed my backpack off the porch. I couldn't think of anything rotten enough to call Chris Hassler. So I spun around and left.

"Zack!" Chris yelled. "You're not really mad, are you?"

I slammed the gate behind me. That's it, I ordered myself. No more falling for stupid ghost stories. Not from Chris. Not from my brother, Kevin. Not from anybody.

I hurried down the street. I noticed jack-o'-lanterns on some porches. And the big oak tree near the corner of Hawthorne Street had little strips of white sheets blowing from its branches.

This Halloween nothing is going to scare me. Nothing.

Chris raced after me. "How long are you going to hold a grudge this time?" he asked, panting.

"Go away," I snapped.

We turned the corner and I spotted the back of my best friend, Marcy Novi. She was headed toward school. Marcy sits in front of me in Miss Prescott's class. Which explains why I'm so good at recognizing her from the back.

I trotted up to her. Chris followed.

"Hi, guys," Marcy said. "Zack, what happened to your jacket?" She pointed to my sleeve.

8

I stared down. A jagged tear ran from my wrist to my elbow.

"Zack saved my life this morning," Chris answered before I could say anything. "He's a hero."

"Really?" Marcy asked, all excited.

"Yep," Chris said. "Zack rescued me from a ghost dog."

Marcy shook her head. "Another dumb joke, huh? And you fell for it, Zack?"

I shrugged.

Marcy doesn't make fun of people. That's one of the reasons she's my best friend. She's a good listener, too. I can really talk to her when something is bugging me.

The three of us hurried up the block and into school. As we reached Miss Prescott's class, the door flew open. Debbie Steinford burst into the hallway. Debbie's the shortest girl in the class. She tries to make up for it by having the biggest hair.

"Aren't you supposed to be going in the other direction?" Marcy asked. "The bell is about to ring."

Debbie shook her head. Her hair whipped my face. "We have a substitute teacher today. She wants new chalk from the supply closet."

"What happened to Miss Prescott?" I asked.

"I don't know," Debbie answered. "Sick, I guess."

Chris grinned. "A substitute. Cool. Let's all drop our books on the floor at nine-thirty. And then—"

"No way," I interrupted.

"But that's what substitutes are for," Chris said. "Don't be such a dweeb."

"Me? A dweeb? Do you think I'm a dweeb, Marcy?" I asked.

"Well, I can't picture you giving a substitute a hard time," Marcy said. "But that doesn't make you a dweeb."

"I bet even Chris will be nice to this sub." Debbie lowered her voice. "She's creepy."

"What do you mean?" I asked. I slid my hand into my backpack and touched the rubber snake. Careful, I told myself.

"I think she's a ghost, Zack," Debbie whispered.

"What's going on?" I demanded. "Is everyone trying to get a head start on Halloween—the official Scare Zack Day? Well, forget it. It's not working."

"But the substitute does look like a ghost," Debbie insisted, her eyes growing wide. "Her skin is so white, you can practically see through it. It's totally weird."

"Then I can't wait to get to class." I pushed past them. "Weird is what I like from now on."

I flung open the door to our classroom.

I choked back a scream.

Our new teacher *was* a ghost.

3

The substitute didn't have a face. Only two dark spots where her eyes should be. And she hovered above the floor.

I glanced around the classroom. Why didn't any of the other kids appear to be scared?

I focused on the substitute again. A veil! She's wearing a veil. That's why I thought she didn't have a face.

And she's not floating. She's wearing a fluffy white skirt that hangs to the floor. And white shoes.

And shiny white gloves. Nothing frightening about that. Strange, yes. Scary, no.

I took a deep breath and crossed the room to my desk. I felt pretty proud of myself. I had managed not to scream. And not to run away. I had remained calm and found the explanation.

Yes! I thought. I am a Power Kid.

I watched the substitute slowly reach up and remove her hat and veil. Her face was very wrinkled. And very pale. It was almost as white as her clothes. And it seemed sort of frozen.

Her scalp showed through her thin white hair. She must be a hundred years old, I thought.

Chris, Marcy, and Debbie entered the room as the bell rang.

"Good morning, boys and girls," the substitute began. "My name is Miss Gaunt. I'll be your teacher until Miss Prescott is feeling better. She's probably going to be out for the entire week. Perhaps in art class we can make a get-well card for her. Now please stand for the Pledge of Allegiance."

As soon as we finished the pledge, Miss Gaunt reached into the top drawer of the desk for Miss Prescott's attendance book.

"Abernathy, Danny," she called in a high, trembly voice.

"Here."

"Here?" she asked as she scanned the room.

"Just here? In my day young boys and girls always addressed their elders by name."

"Here, Miss Gaunt," Danny replied.

"Oh, that's much better, Danny," she said happily.

Miss Gaunt called more names. I noticed that she took the time to say something to each kid after she checked them off in the book.

"Hassler, Christopher."

"Here, Miss Gaunt," Chris called.

"What a good, clear voice you have, Chris," Miss Gaunt commented.

She continued to read out the names. I wonder what she'll say when she gets to me?

"Novi, Marcy."

"Here, Miss Gaunt," Marcy answered.

Miss Gaunt glanced up at Marcy. "What lovely hair you have, my dear."

"Thank you, Miss Gaunt."

"Pepper, Zachariah."

"Here, Miss Gaunt," I said.

"Zachariah. Such a lovely old-fashioned name." She closed her eyes and sighed.

"Everyone calls me Zack, Miss Gaunt," I told her. "Even my mom and dad."

"But you won't mind if I call you Zachariah,

14

will you?" she asked. "You'll be making an old woman very happy, you know."

I felt my ears turn hot. They always do that when I'm embarrassed.

"Sure," I mumbled.

Chris turned around in his seat, grinning at me. And mouthing one word over and over. I didn't have to be an expert lip-reader to know the word was *dweeb*.

When Miss Gaunt finished calling roll, she strolled up and down the aisles. She seemed to be studying us.

As she walked along the last row, next to the windows, a horrible squeaking sound filled the classroom. It made my teeth ache. What is that noise? I wondered.

I glanced over to the window ledge where Homer sits. Homer is our class hamster. He was running on his treadmill. I'd never seen him move so fast. The metal wheel squeaked louder and louder as he ran faster and faster.

What's wrong with him? I thought. We named Homer after Homer Simpson because he's such a couch potato. Walking to his food dish is his total exercise.

That's probably why the wheel is squeaking so much, I realized. It's never been used.

"My, what is he so excited about?" Miss Gaunt stared at Homer.

"Usually he sleeps all day," Marcy told her.

Miss Gaunt moved a few steps closer. She peered into Homer's cage. Homer ran even harder.

Miss Gaunt rapped playfully on the top of the cage.

"Good little hamster," she said softly. "You'll be quiet now, won't you?"

The squeaking sound stopped immediately. Homer jumped off the wheel and plopped down in the sawdust at the bottom of his cage.

Whoa, I thought. Miss Gaunt should open a hamster obedience school. Homer never does anything *I* tell him to.

"What do you children do after attendance?"

Chris's hand flew up. I knew what he was up to. But this time I planned to beat him to it.

I shot my hand up, too.

"Yes, Zachariah?"

"Right after attendance we have recess, Miss Gaunt," I announced. "And right after recess we go to lunch."

Most of the kids laughed. It will be a while before Chris calls me a dweeb again, I thought!

"Oh, I just love a boy with a sense of humor," Miss Gaunt said. "Tell me, Zachariah. Are you so

16

amusing when you stay after school and write 'I Promise Never to Be a Smart Aleck' a hundred times on the blackboard?"

Miss Gaunt snatched up the pointer in the chalk tray. She walked toward my desk. When Chris played tricks on the substitutes, they never punished him. How come it backfired when I tried it?

"Zachariah, you didn't really mean to be so rude, did you?" Miss Gaunt asked. With each word she rapped the pointer on the top of my desk.

"No, Miss Gaunt," I mumbled, watching the pointer.

"I knew that," Miss Gaunt replied. "The moment I saw you, I just knew you were not that kind of boy."

"It's just that I—"

"Oh, you don't need to apologize. Not to me," she said. "You and I are going to get along fine."

Then she placed her fingers under my chin. Forcing me to stare up at her.

"I'll be keeping my eye on you, Zachariah Pepper!"

Even through her gloves, her touch was cold. Ice cold.

17

4

"**O**h, Zach-a-ri-ah!" I heard Chris yell.

I spotted him and Marcy on the other side of the cafeteria. I wove around the long tables, then plopped down on the bench across from them. Chris leaned forward and made loud kissing noises. "Zach-a-ri-ah, such a bea-u-ti-ful name!" he cried in that clear voice Miss Gaunt liked so much.

"So what do you think of Miss Gaunt?" I asked, trying to ignore him.

"I think she needs to be arrested by the fashion police," Tiffany Loomis called from the corner of the table. "Where did she find those clothes?"

"Maybe she thought today was Halloween," Danny Abernathy volunteered.

"Yeah," Tiffany agreed. "But her clothes are even spookier than a Halloween costume."

"Did you notice how pale she is?" I asked. "I wonder if she ever goes out in the sun."

Marcy finished her sandwich. She stared off into space for a moment. Then she said, "Miss Gaunt is kind of strange, but she's really good at teaching things. Like that spelling trick about the word *weird: 'Weird* is weird—it doesn't follow the *i* before *e* except after *c* rule.'"

"She is a pretty good teacher," I said. "But that's probably because she's been teaching forever. She must be a hundred years old."

"You know what I think about Miss Gaunt?" Chris asked. "I think she's in love with Zach-a-riah."

"Cut it out," I snapped back.

"She did pick you to feed Homer this week," Tiffany said, laughing.

I glanced up at the cafeteria clock. Ten minutes till lunch period ended. "I think I'll feed him now. I want to give him part of my apple."

"I'll come, too," Marcy said. "I have a piece of celery left.

19

"I'll help," Chris added. "But he's not getting any of my lunch."

The three of us grabbed our stuff and headed back to our classroom.

"Hello, children," Miss Gaunt called as we trooped in. "What eager students you are. Class doesn't begin for another ten minutes."

"We wanted to feed Homer his lunch," I explained.

"Very conscientious of you, Zachariah," she said.

"Thanks," I muttered. I waited for Chris to start laughing. He didn't. He was staring over my shoulder.

"Look!" he said, pointing. "Something terrible has happened to Homer!"

"Did the ghost dog get him?" I shot back. I couldn't believe Chris thought I'd fall for another one of his stupid jokes so soon.

"I'm not kidding!" Chris declared. "Something weird is going on!"

Marcy peered into Homer's cage. "Chris is right!"

I turned around and stared at the hamster.

Every single hair on Homer's body had turned white.

5

All the kids returned from lunch. We huddled around Homer's cage.

"Maybe someone switched hamsters on us," Chris said. "Maybe it *isn't* Homer."

"Oh, it's Homer, all right," Marcy insisted. "Look at his ear. See the little rip in it? Remember when he had the accident? It's still Homer."

"I've heard of this happening to people if something really scary happens to them," I said. "I didn't know it could happen to animals, too."

But it did happen. And I knew who was to blame.

21

Miss Gaunt.

I remembered how strange Homer acted this morning when she stood near his cage. She must have something to do with this, I thought. She must.

"What's going on here?" Miss Gaunt asked, coming up behind us.

"Homer turned white," Chris explained, stepping back from the cage so Miss Gaunt could see.

The minute Homer spotted Miss Gaunt, his entire body began to shake. And he burrowed his head under some sawdust.

He's trembling, I noticed. Animals are supposed to be good judges of people. And Homer is terrified. Anyone can see that.

Uh-oh, I thought. What if Miss Gaunt really is—a ghost!

"Turning white is not that unusual," Miss Gaunt said, interrupting my thoughts. "Many animals turn white as winter comes. It's their camouflage."

"You mean it protects them from being eaten by other animals?" Danny asked.

Miss Gaunt smiled at him. "Very good, Danny," she said. "It is much more difficult to see a white animal against white snow. And more difficult to see means more difficult to catch—and eat."

"Does anyone know of another animal that changes color in the winter?"

"An ermine?" Marcy called out.

"Well done, Marcy," Miss Gaunt said. "Or it is possible that Homer has a vitamin deficiency. That can often make an animal's fur change color. Perhaps we can ask your science teacher."

When I thought about it, Miss Gaunt's explanations made sense. "Oh, boy. I almost did it again," I muttered. "I almost freaked out over nothing. I have to finish *Power Kids!* tonight."

Miss Gaunt clapped her hands. "Finish feeding Homer, children. We have work to do."

I pulled out the hamster's water bottle and filled it in the sink in the back of the room. Miss Gaunt followed me.

"You seemed very interested in my little science lesson, Zachariah."

I didn't know what to say. I spied Chris staring at us. His mouth curled up in his stupid grin.

Miss Gaunt didn't wait for an answer. "I enjoy teaching so much more when I have an enthusiastic student," she told me.

I nodded quickly and hurried back to Homer's

cage with the bottle. On the way I passed Chris's seat. "Here comes the teacher's pet," he whispered to Tiffany. She giggled.

By the time I returned to my desk, Miss Gaunt had started the history lesson. "This afternoon we will continue your study of the American Revolution," she announced. She opened a box and dumped a bunch of old metal soldiers on her desk.

"Danny, I would like you to lead the British," she instructed. "Come collect your soldiers."

As Danny headed toward the front of the room, Miss Gaunt asked, "Who would like to take the role of George Washington?" Lots of kids raised their hands. Her eyes searched the room.

I stared down at my desk. The soldiers looked like fun, but I didn't want to get chosen for anything. Not by her.

"Zachariah, would you lead the rebel forces?" she called.

I heard Chris snicker.

I shuffled up to Miss Gaunt's desk and gathered up a handful of soldiers.

That's when I noticed something on the side of Miss Gaunt's neck. A deep purple blotch. Kind of long and bumpy.

I didn't want Miss Gaunt to notice me staring. I

24

glanced down at my soldiers. Then I stole another quick peek.

The thing on Miss Gaunt's neck moved.

It was alive!

Miss Gaunt had a fat, slimy worm crawling on her neck!

6

The worm was thick and wet looking. I watched as Miss Gaunt reached up and picked it off her neck. Then she squooshed it between her gloved fingers and tossed it into the wastebasket.

I glanced at the other kids. They were all gathered around a huge map Miss Gaunt had spread on the floor. No one had noticed a thing.

Maybe it was a piece of fuzz, I tried to convince myself. But I didn't think so.

I didn't talk to anybody the rest of the afternoon. After history we made a card for Miss Prescott. Then it was time to go home.

Marcy, Chris, and I left school together. But I

didn't say anything to them about what I had seen.

That night I made sure I finished reading *Power Kids!*

Okay, Zack, I told myself as I opened the classroom door the next morning, it's power time. You did *not* see a worm on Miss Gaunt's neck yesterday. Remember what *Power Kids!* said: You see what you expect to see.

And you always expect to see something scary, I reminded myself.

But not anymore!

I calmly walked over to my desk and sat down. I studied Miss Gaunt's neck carefully. Pasty white skin. Nothing else. No worm.

Miss Gaunt took the attendance and I began to relax. We said the Pledge of Allegiance.

Then we began a math lesson. "Who would like to go to the blackboard and show the class how to multiply decimals?" Miss Gaunt asked.

I tried to make myself invisible. I scrunched down in my chair. I was safe. Lots of kids waved their hands.

"How about you showing us, Zachariah?" Miss Gaunt suggested.

"Actually, I'm not all that good at decimals, Miss Gaunt," I admitted.

27

"That's why we come to school, isn't it?" Miss Gaunt asked. "So we can learn to do better?"

"But you see, I'm not—" I began, but my mouth grew dry. My voice cracked.

"Not feeling well, dear?" Miss Gaunt asked in her high little voice. "You're not coming down with a sore throat, are you?" She walked down the aisle toward me. "Do you need to see the school nurse?"

She reached out to press her hand on my forehead.

"Honest, Miss Gaunt," I said, pulling away. "I'm fine." I didn't want to feel the touch of her icy fingers again.

Miss Gaunt stretched out her hand once more. Her white glove smelled a little like dirt. And it looked grimy.

As she placed her hand on my forehead, I remembered how cold my grandmother's hands were sometimes. Grandma said it was because of poor circulation—it happens when people get older.

I forced myself to sit still. Miss Gaunt couldn't help that her hands were cold.

But when she touched me, I felt the cold all the way inside my head. A sharp stinging pain.

"Well, you don't have a fever, Zachariah," Miss

28

Gaunt said. "Could it be that you're afraid of making a mistake—and the other children teasing you?"

I shrugged. "I don't understand decimals at all."

"Well, no one's going to laugh at you, Zachariah. Not in my classroom. Besides, I never met a Zachariah who didn't multiply decimals beautifully!"

I glanced around the room. None of the kids seemed as if they were about to laugh. Not even Chris. But even if they didn't laugh now, I knew they'd make fun of me after school.

But I had no choice. I approached the chalkboard.

"Thirty-seven point twenty-nine multiplied by four hundred and seventy-two point sixty-three," Miss Gaunt instructed. "Write it on the blackboard, Zachariah."

My hand trembled. I could barely write out the numbers.

"Go ahead," she said. "Now write down the answer."

I swallowed hard. "I can't," I said quietly.

"Why is that, Zachariah?" Miss Gaunt asked.

"Because I don't know how." Is Miss Gaunt going to make me stand up here all day? I was beginning to panic. I felt my ears turn hot.

29

"You can do it, Zachariah," Miss Gaunt said firmly. "I know you can, dear."

She stepped toward me.

Squeak. Squeak. Squeak. I heard Homer in his cage. Running wildly on his treadmill again.

"Be still, Homer," Miss Gaunt called. "Let Zachariah concentrate now."

The squeaking stopped abruptly.

My hand floated into the air. I squeezed the chalk between my fingers, but I didn't feel anything. My fingers were numb.

What's happening? It felt as though a big magnet was tugging my hand up. Up to the chalkboard.

Then I began to write. My hand wrote number after number.

"Very good, Zachariah," Miss Gaunt said proudly. "I knew you could do it."

But I knew I didn't do it. Something else did.

Something else had control of my arm!

7

My arm flopped back to my side. The chalk flew from my fingers. It broke against the floor.

"Well done, Zachariah," Miss Gaunt said. "You may return to your seat."

I stumbled down the aisle to my desk and slid into the chair. My arm felt itchy. Prickly.

I stared down at my hand and wiggled my fingers.

I raised my eyes to Miss Gaunt. She smiled at me proudly—and winked.

She did it, I thought. Miss Gaunt forced me to write the correct answer. She moved my hand!

Power Kids! didn't cover anything like this. I

31

had to tell Marcy and Chris. This wasn't my imagination. This was for real.

When the lunch bell finally rang, I bolted out the door. I waited a few feet down the hall for Marcy and Chris.

"You did great in math," Marcy called when she spotted me.

"Yeah," Chris agreed.

"It wasn't me," I told them.

"What do you mean?" Chris asked.

I motioned for them to move away from the door. I didn't want Miss Gaunt—or anyone else—to hear what I had to say.

"It wasn't me," I repeated. "I didn't know the answers, and I didn't move my hand."

"What?" Chris demanded.

"Miss Gaunt took control of me. She made my hand move," I whispered. "She's a ghost. I know it."

Chris clutched his chest and staggered back a few steps. "No!" he cried. Then he started to laugh.

"Come on, Zack," Marcy pleaded.

"Think about it," I insisted. "Homer turned white on the day she started. Your hair turns white when you get scared, right?"

32

"My mother said her hair turned white the day she had me," Chris joked.

Marcy ignored him. "Miss Gaunt explained about Homer turning white, remember? Camouflage or vitamin deficiency."

"But other strange things have happened, too," I insisted.

"Yeah," Chris chimed in. "Don't forget—Zack got the right answer to a decimal question!"

Marcy slapped Chris on the shoulder.

"He's right, Marcy. I didn't know the answer. I'm telling you—she moved my hand! And there's something else," I said. "I saw a worm on Miss Gaunt's neck yesterday, and it didn't even bother her. She just squooshed it."

"Gross!" Marcy exclaimed.

"Cool," Chris added.

"So what are we going to do about Miss Gaunt?" I asked.

"Bring her some Worms-Away?" Chris suggested. "That's what we give my cousin's dog."

I didn't really expect any help from Chris. But what would Marcy say?

Marcy shook her head. "She *is* really creepy, Zack. But she's not a ghost. There's no such thing as ghosts."

Not even Marcy—my best friend—believed me. What was I going to do?

Marcy grabbed my arm and pulled me down the hall. "Let's go eat. Maybe you'll feel better after lunch."

"I'm so hungry I could eat a ghost horse," Chris said as he followed us to the cafeteria.

I stopped suddenly.

"What's wrong?" Marcy asked.

"Nothing. I left my lunch in my desk. I'll meet you guys inside."

I dashed down the hall. If Miss Gaunt is still in the classroom, I'll skip lunch, I thought. Because I'm definitely not going in there alone.

I peeked inside. The room was empty.

I hurried to my desk and opened the top.

Something white fluttered to the ground.

It was one of Miss Gaunt's gloves!

8

Why was Miss Gaunt's glove in my desk? I wondered. She must have been snooping around, I guessed. And dropped it there by accident.

I didn't say anything about the glove to Marcy or Chris during lunch. In fact, I didn't say much of anything. I didn't really feel like talking.

After lunch we piled into the classroom. Chris's hand shot up before Miss Gaunt could say a word.

Oh, no. I stiffened in my seat. He's going to tell everyone what I said. He's going to tell them Miss Gaunt is a ghost.

"Miss Gaunt," Chris began. "Halloween is coming up—"

I sank down. And let out a long sigh.

"And Miss Prescott said we could have a party on Friday," Chris announced.

"Then we shall have one," Miss Gaunt told him. "Thank you for bringing it up, Chris."

Miss Gaunt turned to the chalkboard. "Let's begin with a list of what we need."

"Cookies," Debbie called out.

Miss Gaunt started to write on the board. The chalk snapped and fell from her fingers. Bobby Dreyfuss picked it up for her. He sat in the front row.

I could hardly read the words she wrote. The letters were all different sizes. And very wobbly.

"Decorations," Marcy suggested.

The chalk screeched across the board as Miss Gaunt continued the list. She dropped the chalk again.

"Is something wrong with your hand?" Bobby asked as he picked up the chalk again and handed it to Miss Gaunt.

"It's just a little arthritis," Miss Gaunt said. "It happens when we get older."

"Do you have arthritis in your other hand, too, Miss Gaunt?" Bobby asked.

I noticed that Miss Gaunt held her right hand tucked inside her blouse. Doesn't she usually write with that hand? I thought she did, but I couldn't remember.

"Why don't we keep our attention on what we need for the party," Miss Gaunt suggested.

"But I only—" Bobby started.

"Please, Bobby," Miss Gaunt said stiffly. "Let's go on with the list."

Miss Gaunt dropped the chalk in the tray. "Perhaps we don't need a list. Debbie, would you like to volunteer for the liquid refreshment?" she asked.

"You mean drinks?" Debbie asked uncertainly.

"Exactly, dear," Miss Gaunt replied. "People enjoy cider at Halloween parties. Do you think you could manage that?"

"Yes, Miss Gaunt," Debbie said.

"How about cups and plates?"

Danny waved his hand in the air. "My dad works over at Dalby's," he told her. "He can get them for us free, I bet."

"Why, how nice," Miss Gaunt said. "Will you thank your father for us?"

"Can we play games?" Chris asked. "We've been collecting money to buy some."

"What kinds of games did you have in mind, Chris?" Miss Gaunt asked. "Something like Pin the Tail on the Donkey?"

"More like Pin the Fangs on the Werewolf," Chris said. "Or how about Dead Man's Bluff?"

"That sounds a bit frightening, doesn't it?" Miss Gaunt asked. "Do you children really enjoy these games?"

"It's Halloween," Chris insisted. "It's supposed to be scary. I bet we could find some cool games down at Dalby's."

"Why don't you try Shop Till You Drop," Miss Gaunt said. "It's a new place over by the Stop 'N' Shop. Take Zack and Marcy with you. They can help pick out decorations there. But nothing too horrifying, please."

The last bell rang. I leaped out of my chair and headed for the door.

"Would you stay behind, Zachariah?" Miss Gaunt called.

"Just me?" I asked.

"Don't worry," she said. "I only want to ask you a little question, dear."

Miss Gaunt waited until everyone left the classroom. Then she closed the door and turned toward me.

"May I have it?" she asked.

"Have *what*, Miss Gaunt?"

"You have something that belongs to me, Zachariah," she stated.

38

"I didn't take anything," I said. "Honest."

"But I saw you put it in your pocket, dear," she said. "It should still be there."

I stuck my hand into my pocket. Her glove. I forgot that I shoved it in there.

I pulled the glove out. It slipped from my fingers and fluttered to the floor.

"Do you think you could pick that up for me, Zachariah?" Miss Gaunt asked.

As I bent over I said, "I'm sorry about your arthritis, Miss Gaunt." Then I held the glove out to her.

"What arthritis, dear?"

"But you told Bobby—"

"Oh, Bobby is so nosy," Miss Gaunt declared. "I had to tell him something, didn't I?"

She reached for the glove with her left hand. Then she whipped her right hand out from the fold of her blouse.

And there wasn't any skin on her fingers!

Only bones.

The bones of a skeleton.

9

"**H**er hand—it was horrible," I told Chris and Marcy. "It didn't have any skin on it."

My knees began to buckle as I described it.

We were on our way to the party decoration store—the one Miss Gaunt told us about.

"And we shouldn't go to this store," I added. "We shouldn't do anything Miss Gaunt tells us to do."

"Get a grip," Chris said.

"How long did you see her hand for, anyway?"

"Just for a second," I admitted. "Until she put her glove back on. But that was long enough. I'm telling you—Miss Gaunt is a ghost."

"Come on, Zack. That's what happens when people grow old," Marcy explained. "They get very thin."

"It wasn't just thin," I insisted. "It was bony—like a real skeleton's hand!"

"Look! There it is," Chris said, pointing. "The party store."

I gazed across the street. There it was, all right. Miss Gaunt said its name was Shop Till You Drop. But the sign out front read Shop Till You Drop *Dead*.

"Oooooo. There could be ghosts inside, Zack!" Chris joked when he noticed the sign. "Are you sure you want to go in?"

"Don't be an idiot, Chris," Marcy replied, crossing the street.

"I don't think it's open," I said as we neared the store. "I don't see any lights on."

Marcy was the first to reach the front door. "Oh, I get it," she said. "Someone's painted the windows black." She pressed her face against the glass. She cupped her hands around her eyes. "I can't see anything in there."

She pushed on the door. It opened silently.

Inside a single dirty bulb hung from the ceiling. It swung back and forth, back and forth—casting creepy shadows on the walls.

The store appeared to be huge—but it was hard to tell in the dim light. It also appeared to be empty.

"Hello! Is anybody here?" Chris yelled. No one answered.

The door banged shut behind us.

"Anybody here?" Chris called again.

I heard a soft rustling sound. Then silence.

My eyes adjusted to the darkness. The store was lined with tall wooden shelves that stretched almost to the ceiling. Beyond them, the back of the store was bathed in a deep purple glow.

"Let's go to Dalby's," Marcy said. "This place *is* creepy."

"Yeah," I agreed.

"I want to stay," Chris argued. "I bet we can find some cool Halloween stuff here. Besides, I promised my mom I'd be home by four. I don't have time to go to another place."

Chris hurried down one of the narrow aisles.

I followed him. I didn't want him telling everyone in school that I freaked out in a Halloween store.

Everything smelled strange. Kind of moldy—like old mushrooms. And the floor felt bumpy and uneven. I heard something crunch under my feet.

"How are we supposed to find anything when

we can't *see* anything?" Marcy muttered behind me.

We took a few more steps.

Crunch, crunch, crunch.

"What is making that noise?" Marcy asked.

I stared down at the floor. "I can't tell," I answered. "It sounds like we're walking on peanut shells or something."

I crouched down, peered at my shoes—and saw them. Millions of them.

Millions of slimy black beetles swarming all over the floor.

Marcy spotted them, too. We both gasped.

Suddenly a bright overhead light flashed on. Marcy kneeled to study the beetles. Then she picked one up!

"Plastic," she announced. "Plastic bugs."

"Uh, I guess they decorated the whole store for Halloween," I said. "Pretty cool, huh?"

We both laughed.

"Hey, Marcy, the light that went on—who threw the switch?" I asked. We both glanced around. No one was in sight.

"Where's Chris?" Marcy asked.

"He was right in front of me a minute ago," I told her.

I figured Chris was probably hiding down one of

the aisles. Waiting to jump out at us. Well, he's not going to get me this time, I told myself. I scanned the shelves, searching for something creepy to use to scare him first.

The shelves were crammed with all kinds of strange stuff. A jar full of glass eyeballs. A withered hand. A mesh bag filled with small bones. And some cool masks.

I grabbed two masks. I pulled a gorilla mask over my head. It smelled rotten inside—like spoiled meat. But I didn't care.

I handed the other mask to Marcy. It was really gross. A monster face with one eyeball hanging from a bloody thread.

"Chris!" I shouted as loud as I could. "Where are you?"

Then I leaned in close to Marcy and whispered, "I bet Chris is hiding around that corner. Let's scare him before he can scare us."

Marcy smiled and slipped the mask over her head.

We tiptoed to the end of the aisle. I hope Chris doesn't hear those stupid plastic bugs crunching, I thought.

I turned to Marcy and held up three fingers. She nodded. We'd both jump around the corner on the count of three.

I gave the signal and leaped out. I beat on my chest and howled.

Marcy screeched—high and long. I was impressed. She really sounded scary.

Someone *was* standing around that corner, but it wasn't Chris. It was a man. The strangest man I had ever seen. His head was big and round—the size of a basketball. The pasty skin on his face stretched right up over his bald scalp. He wore a shiny black cape that trailed to the floor.

Marcy dug her fingernails into my arm and pointed—to something lying on the ground at the man's feet.

It was Chris. Lying absolutely still.

A trickle of blood ran from the corner of his mouth.

10

~~~

"**W**hat did you do to Chris!" I screamed. Marcy and I ripped off our masks and fell to Chris's side.

"Chris!" Marcy cried. "Chris, are you okay?"

Chris's eyes fluttered. He struggled to sit up. Then he cried, "Gotcha!"

Marcy and I glared at him.

"Come on, guys. Say something," Chris whined. "Hey, don't you think this fake blood is great?"

"Yes, it is delicious, isn't it?" the bald man replied.

Chris jerked his head back. "Who are you?" he asked, scrambling to his feet.

"I?" the man asked. "Why, I am Mr. Sangfwad.

The owner of this establishment. How may I serve you?" He stroked the head of a small, furry animal buried in his arms.

"We're here for Halloween," Chris mumbled.

"To buy games and decorations for our class party," Marcy added.

"Oh, oh, oh!" Mr. Sangfwad exclaimed. "Evangeline must have sent you!" Then he grinned, showing off a big dark hole where his two front teeth used to be.

"Evangeline?" Chris asked.

"From Shadyside Middle School," Mr. Sangfwad explained. "The substitute teacher."

"Oh!" I groaned. "You must mean Miss Gaunt."

"Yes. Yes. Miss Gaunt. And you must be Zachariah," Mr. Sangfwad said, studying me carefully. "Evangeline speaks very highly of you."

"Do you really know Miss Gaunt?" I asked.

"Why, of course I do. Miss Gaunt and I have been friends in Shadyside forever. Haven't we, Phoebe?" he crooned to the little gray pet in his arms.

"But I've lived here my whole life," I said. "I've never seen either of you before."

"Life is strange, isn't it?" Mr. Sangfwad replied.

47

That wasn't exactly the answer I was looking for.

With both hands Mr. Sangfwad lifted his pet high in the air.

Its tiny black eyes popped into view.

Then its whiskers.

Then its sharp yellow teeth.

A rat!

"You're holding a rat!" I cried.

"Oh, don't let Phoebe scare you." Mr. Sangfwad kissed the top of the rat's head. "She's quite sweet."

"She could bite you!" Chris warned.

"Rats will be rats," Mr. Sangfwad said.

"You could die!" Marcy exclaimed.

"I said she was sweet," Mr. Sangfwad replied. "I didn't say she was harmless!"

Mr. Sangfwad placed Phoebe on the floor. I hoped she would scurry away. But instead she circled our feet.

"Now. Exactly what kind of games would you like for your Halloween party?" Mr. Sangfwad asked.

"Do you have Pin the Fangs on the Werewolf and Dead Man's Bluff?" Chris asked.

"Why, of course," Mr. Sangfwad answered. "They are in aisle three, and—" Chris headed

48

over to the aisle before Mr. Sangfwad finished. "Don't forget Spin the Zombie and Power Ghouls," he called after him.

"Do you have Halloween decorations?" Marcy asked politely.

"Halloween decorations? For Evangeline's students? Of course I do. I suppose you want black and orange streamers—that sort of thing."

"Exactly," I told him. I couldn't wait to leave the store. Mr. Sangfwad gave me the creeps.

When we had everything we needed, Marcy and I met Chris at the cash register.

Mr. Sangfwad rang up the order. Marcy paid him with the money we had collected in school.

"I'm afraid I've run out of bags," Mr. Sangfwad announced, searching under the counter. "I have some in back if you would wait just a moment."

Chris checked his watch. "It's ten to four. I've gotta go. My mom will kill me if I'm not home on time today."

"Go ahead," Marcy told him. "Zack and I can handle this stuff."

"Great." Chris hurried out the front door. "See ya!"

Marcy and I waited by the cash register. I shifted from one foot to the other. I wanted to get out of there.

"What's taking him so long?" I complained.

"He just left," Marcy said. "Be patient."

I kept checking my watch. "Maybe we can carry this stuff without bags," I suggested. "We've already paid. Let's go."

"Shhh," Marcy whispered. "Here he comes."

"Okeydokey," Mr. Sangfwad sang out cheerfully, approaching the counter. He piled all our decorations into a bag.

"Now, are you sure you have everything you need for your party?" he asked. "Halloween is very, very important to Evangeline."

Then he stared directly into my eyes and added, "I know *you* wouldn't want to disappoint her."

"**W**ell?" I demanded once we stepped outside. "Do you believe me now?"

"Do I believe what?" Marcy asked.

"That Miss Gaunt is a ghost," I shot back.

"Zack, you're being ridiculous."

"How can you say that?" I practically shrieked. "Everything about her is totally weird—including her creepy friend Mr. Sangfwad and his horrible store."

"Mr. Sangfwad was kind of strange. . . ." Marcy's voice trailed off.

"Kind of strange?" I screeched. "He had a rat for a pet! And didn't you hear what he said—that

he and Miss Gaunt have lived in Shadyside *forever?*"

"So, what's your point?" Marcy asked.

"Don't you think it's kind of funny that we've never seen either of them before?"

"Well . . ." Marcy began.

"Come with me after school tomorrow," I interrupted. "I'm going to follow Miss Gaunt. And I'm going to get real proof."

"Fine," Marcy said.

"Then—you mean—you believe me?" I asked excitedly.

"No," Marcy replied. "I'm going with you to prove once and for all that there are no such things as ghosts!"

"She *is* a ghost, Marcy. You'll see!"

Was I right? Was Miss Gaunt really a ghost?

I wasn't sure of anything anymore.

But we were going to follow her. And we were finally going to find out.

I had no idea what my decision would lead to.

12

The next morning we rode our bikes to school. We'd use them afterward to follow Miss Gaunt.

I couldn't wait for the final bell to ring. But by the end of the day, I began to feel scared. What if Miss Gaunt caught us following her?

Even if she wasn't a ghost, she'd be pretty angry. And we'd be in tons of trouble.

If she was a ghost, things could be a lot worse.

What did ghosts do to people who stumbled in their way?

I didn't know. And I didn't want to find out.

After the last bell rang, Marcy and I hid alongside the school trophy case in the front hall. We watched all the kids leave.

Then Miss Gaunt appeared. She approached the school's two heavy steel front doors. I noticed how tiny and frail she seemed in front of them. I wondered if she would have trouble opening them. I always do. But when she grabbed the exit bar and pushed, the door flew open.

"Did you see that?" I whispered to Marcy. "Did you see how easily she opened the door? Now what do you think?"

Marcy stared at me—as if I were nuts.

No sense in starting an argument with her, I decided. We would both find out the truth soon enough.

When the door swung closed, we crept over to it. We opened it a crack and watched Miss Gaunt climb down the steps.

She headed across the school yard. Then she ducked behind some bushes. We dashed outside.

"Oh, no!" I cried. "We've lost her already!"

"No, we haven't," Marcy said, jabbing me in the ribs.

She was right. There was Miss Gaunt—out from behind the bushes. Pedaling a bike!

"I can't believe Miss Gaunt rides a bike," I said as we ran over to ours. "She's too old for that."

We leaped on our bikes and charged after her.

By the time we reached the first intersection, Miss Gaunt had disappeared.

"Do you think she turned left or right on Park Drive?" Marcy asked.

"I don't know. We'll just have to guess."

The light turned green, and we turned right on Park. There was Miss Gaunt—directly ahead of us. "Yes!" I cried.

Miss Gaunt turned right again. Onto Fear Street.

I remembered what my brother, Kevin, told me about Fear Street—that the most evil ghosts of all haunted it.

"It figures," I moaned to Marcy. "Miss Gaunt lives on Fear Street."

"Even if she does live on Fear Street, that doesn't mean she's a ghost," Marcy said firmly.

We rode by the houses on Fear Street. Some of them were all fixed up. A lot of them were wrecks, with sagging porches and peeling paint.

And some were totally abandoned. Looming above all of them was the burned-out shell of the Fear mansion. That one was definitely the scariest.

We pedaled quickly by the mansion. Following Miss Gaunt around one curve after another.

The afternoon sun was beginning to set. Fear Street was really spooky in the dark. And we didn't see a single car going in either direction. No joggers. No other bikes. No people out for a stroll.

My head began to throb. It was too scary here. I wanted to turn around and go home.

I was about to suggest it, but Marcy spoke first. "Look! She's slowing down."

"I bet we're coming to her house!" I exclaimed.

I watched Miss Gaunt slip off her bike.

She leaned it against two huge iron gates.

The gates of the Fear Street Cemetery!

13

I slowly reached out and pushed open the iron gate. It felt as cold as Miss Gaunt's fingers.

I glanced over at Marcy. I could tell she was waiting for me to go in first. "So what do you think now?" I asked her.

"People visit graveyards, you know," Marcy replied. But I thought I heard a little quiver in her voice.

I slipped through the gate, Marcy right behind me. I felt like an intruder. The stone angels seemed to stare down at me disapprovingly.

We ran from grave to grave. Ducking behind each tombstone before we sprinted to the next. We had to be very careful. We definitely did not want Miss Gaunt to spot us.

A sudden gust of wind set the autumn leaves swirling. Swirling around the tombstones.

The last rays of the sun had faded. And I shivered in the blast of chilly air.

Miss Gaunt glided between the graves. Marcy and I followed.

"Zack," Marcy whispered, pointing to the ground. "Look!"

I glanced down. A whirling gray mist covered our feet. "Hey! Where did that come from?"

The mist slowly rose to our knees. We watched as it grew thicker. And higher.

"Maybe we should head back," I said anxiously. Then I changed my mind. "No, we can't. We've got to follow Miss Gaunt!"

But when I gazed up, Miss Gaunt had disappeared!

"Where did she go?" I cried.

"I don't know," Marcy replied, squinting to see through the churning gray spray. "The mist is too thick. I think we should go back."

"Okay. Okay," I agreed. "But which way is back?"

"Just follow me," Marcy replied. Then she broke into a run, dashing between the gravestones.

"Slow down, Marcy!" I cried out, trying to keep up.

Marcy tripped over something—probably a rock. I couldn't tell. The mist covered everything now. She hit the ground with a soft thud. But in a second she was up again, running faster.

"Marcy!" I cried out. "Slow down. I'm going to lose you."

Marcy stumbled once more.

I spotted her arms waving frantically through the mist.

"Zack!" she screamed. "Help me!"

Then she sank totally out of sight.

I waited. Waited for her to jump up—so I would know which way to go.

But Marcy didn't appear.

"Marcy!" I yelled. "Where are you?"

Marcy had vanished.

14

"**M**arcy!" I called out, louder this time. "Marcy!"

No answer.

I inched forward.

The mist swirled all around me now. It was impossible to see.

Where was Marcy? Had she run into Miss Gaunt? Did Miss Gaunt have her trapped right now?

My heart hammered away in my chest. The mist had grown icy, and I began to shiver. But I pressed on, calling Marcy's name out every few steps.

"Marcy! Where are you? Marcy!"

"Over here, Zack!"

Marcy!

I stepped in the direction of her voice—and my legs flew out from under me.

I plunged down—down into total darkness.

And then, finally, I landed—somewhere damp and very, very dark.

"Oooh," I groaned, rubbing my head.

As I fumbled to sit up, a cold hand groped in the darkness and grabbed my arm.

"Let me go!" I screamed, trying desperately to shake loose.

"Zack! Stop it! It's me."

"Marcy!" I cried with relief. "Where are we?"

"I think we've fallen into a grave."

"A grave? Oh, gross!" I shouted. "Are we—are we alone down here?"

"Of course we're alone down here," Marcy snapped. "That's why we fell. We fell into an empty grave."

"Okay. Okay," I said. "I just thought that . . . maybe . . . Miss Gaunt was down here, too."

"Zack, she was headed in the other direction when we lost her."

"Oh. Right," I said.

Marcy sighed.

"It's really disgusting down here," I said, glancing around the underground pit. "How are we going to get out?"

"Good question," Marcy replied.

I stood up. Then Marcy and I tried to fling ourselves out of the grave.

But the walls were too high.

We searched the sides of the grave for a rock, a tree root, something to grab on to—to hoist ourselves up. But the dirt simply slipped through our fingers.

"Hey, I have an idea," I said to Marcy. "Give me a boost. Once I'm out, I can help pull you up."

Marcy knit her hands together. I slipped my foot into them and pushed off with all my might. My hands flew up and found the grave opening.

"I'm out!" I shouted.

I hung from the grave's edge, my feet dangling below. Marcy shoved my legs up as I pulled myself to the ground above.

Then I leaned over and dragged Marcy up.

Marcy tumbled out, and we both toppled backward onto the ground.

"Oh, no," Marcy moaned.

"Are you hurt?" I asked.

Marcy didn't answer my question. She simply

stared ahead. And even in the dark I could see she was trembling. Finally she said,

"Read it, Zack."

Marcy was staring at a gravestone. The gravestone at the head of the empty grave.

It was very old.

I could barely make out the engraving.

I moved up close to it, squinted, and read:

EVANGELINE GAUNT
BORN 1769   DIED 1845
REST IN PEACE

"It's *her* grave!" I screamed. "We were in *her* grave!"

15

"She *is* a ghost!" I cried. "Let's get out of here. Before she finds us!"

We charged through the cemetery, stumbling over rocks and dodging graves.

We ran and ran. But we were nowhere near the entrance.

"It's a maze!" Marcy cried. "We're going around in circles."

I stopped. My eyes darted left and right. Trying to find a clue to guide us.

The mist began to lift, and I spotted some hedges a few feet away. "Let's go through there!" I cried.

I parted the hedges and held them back so Marcy could squeeze through. The little thorns ripped into my hands. But I didn't care.

As I shoved through the hedge after Marcy, I yelled, "Look! The entrance! We're almost there!"

We dashed to the gates, jumped on our bikes, and pedaled as hard as we could. We didn't speak until we reached Marcy's house.

"*Now* do you believe me?"

Marcy nodded, gasping for breath. "Miss Gaunt is a ghost. What are we going to do?"

I wiped the sweat from my forehead. "We have to tell the rest of the kids as soon as we reach school tomorrow," I said. "Meet me outside the main entrance at eight-fifteen. We'll catch them before they go in—and warn them. . . ."

I paced back and forth the next morning in front of the school. I glanced at my watch for the hundreth time—8:25 . . . 8:27 . . . 8:31 . . .

Not it was 8:45 and still no Marcy.

Where could she be? I wondered. Most of the kids had arrived and gone inside.

I didn't stop them.

I didn't want to tell them about Miss Gaunt alone. I told Marcy we would do it together.

Besides, I knew no one would believe *me*. I needed Marcy there.

I glanced at my watch one last time—9:00.

I had to go in.

But now I was worried—really worried about Marcy.

Where was she?

Did Miss Gaunt see us yesterday?

Did she know we were following her?

Did she find Marcy this morning and do something horrible to her?

I bolted through the classroom door just as Miss Gaunt began taking attendance. I shot a glance at Marcy's seat. It was empty.

"Abernathy, Danny."

"Here, Miss Gaunt."

I studied Miss Gaunt as she called roll. Her high little voice sounded the same as always. She didn't seem upset—or angry.

"Hassler, Chris."

"Here, Miss Gaunt."

I wondered if Miss Gaunt could tell how upset *I* was.

I held my breath until Miss Gaunt reached Marcy's name.

"Novi, Marcy."

No answer.

"Can anyone tell me why Marcy Novi is not here this morning?" she asked.

No one volunteered.

"Oh, I just remembered," Miss Gaunt said. "Marcy's out for a few days, I'm afraid."

"Is she sick, Miss Gaunt?" Tiffany asked. "Should we send her a card?"

"I doubt it would reach her in time," Miss Gaunt said.

"In time for what?" Tiffany asked.

In time for what?

Suddenly my hands began to shake.

"Really, Tiffany," Miss Gaunt replied. "Would you like to hear someone telling the whole class your family secrets?"

"It's a *secret?*" Tiffany asked excitedly.

Miss Gaunt shook her head in disapproval. Then she continued on.

"Reynolds," she called out sharply.

"Here, Miss Gaunt!"

"Steinford."

"Here, Miss Gaunt!"

Marcy was in trouble. I have to find her, I thought. And fast!

I didn't hear a word Miss Gaunt said all morning. All I could think about was Marcy. I couldn't wait for the lunch bell to ring.

67

The minute it sounded I was halfway to the door.

"Hey, Zack," Danny called out. "You want me to save a seat for you in the cafeteria?"

"Sure, Danny," I answered. I wasn't going to the cafeteria. But I didn't want anyone to know that I was leaving school in the middle of the day.

When I was sure no one was watching, I slipped through the front door and burst outside.

I raced down Hawthorne Street to Canyon Drive.

I ran so hard I thought my lungs would burst. But I didn't stop. There was no time.

I reached Marcy's house in under five minutes.

And as I neared her front gate, I knew something was wrong.

The front door banged open and shut in the wind.

I sprinted up the walk.

Yes. Something was definitely wrong.

The glass in the big front window—it was totally shattered!

16

A man walked out the front door. A stranger with a dark brown beard. He wore a tool belt around his waist.

"Who are you?" I blurted. "Where are the Novis?"

"I'm from the glass company," the man told me. "I'm here to fix the window."

"Where is everyone?"

"The whole family left this morning," the man answered. He measured the new glass. "Some kind of family emergency."

"What kind of emergency?" I demanded.

"An emergency is all my boss told me," the man said.

"Do you know who broke the window?" I asked.

"No," he said, shaking his head. "But it's too bad. A window this big is hard to replace."

"Do you think it could have been some kind of explosion?" I asked.

"Could have been, I suppose," the man replied. "But when I checked the gas line, there was no sign of a leak. Kind of funny, isn't it?"

It wasn't funny at all.

I knew who was responsible.

Miss Gaunt.

What did she do to Marcy's family?

Suddenly I felt sick.

I wanted to go home.

But I couldn't. I had to warn my friends in school. I had to tell them how dangerous Miss Gaunt was.

I barely made it back to Shadyside Middle before the bell rang. Miss Gaunt brought the class to order.

I waited for a good time to write a note to Chris. But Miss Gaunt was staring at me every time I looked up. She kept her eyes on me all through geography and math.

"We'll spend the last hour on spelling," Miss Gaunt announced.

"Miss Prescott always teaches social studies on Tuesday afternoon," Tiffany complained.

"What is it you like so much about social studies, dear?"

"We were studying crop rotation," Tiffany said. "I liked reading about farmers—and how they keep feeding the soil to make things grow better."

"A sweet girl like you interested in dirt?" Miss Gaunt asked. "Why not wait till you're older to study nasty things like that?"

"Does that mean no social studies?" Tiffany asked.

"Not as long as I'm in charge," Miss Gaunt replied. "But how would you like to spell *rotation* for us?"

Tiffany sighed and walked up to the blackboard.

I knew I couldn't wait any longer.

It was time to spread the word about Miss Gaunt.

I ripped a sheet of paper from my notebook.

"Miss Gaunt is a ghost," I wrote. "I have proof. Be very carefull." I folded the paper and wrote Chris's name on the outside.

The seat in front of me was empty—Marcy's

71

seat. So I slipped the note to Debbie Steinford to my right. She's the class goody-goody, but I didn't think she'd tell Miss Gaunt.

Debbie shot me a dirty look, but she grabbed the note anyway. I watched her read Chris's name.

As Miss Gaunt watched Tiffany finish writing *rotation* on the board, Debbie passed the note to Ezra Goldstein in the row ahead of her.

Ezra passed the note to Danny Abernathy ahead of him.

Chris sat in the first row. I held my breath as Danny passed the note to him.

My eyes were glued to Chris as he unfolded the note under his desk.

He pushed his chair back.

Then he bent over to steal a better glimpse. When that didn't work, he spread the note out flat on top of his desk.

I saw him shake his head.

Then he turned around in his chair and flashed me that big stupid grin of his!

I checked the front of the class. Miss Gaunt had called Bobby Dreyfuss up to the board. He was trying to spell *artichoke.*

"A-R-T-A," Bobby spelled aloud as he wrote.

I heard someone snicker. A familiar snicker. Chris, of course.

"Christopher?" Miss Gaunt asked, looming over him. "What's that on you're desk?"

"It's nothing, Miss Gaunt," Chris said. He shoved the note in his pocket.

Bang! Bang! Bang!

Miss Gaunt slammed her pointer on his desk.

"Christopher!" she demanded. "Give me that note!"

17

Don't let me down, Chris! I thought. Just this once, keep your big mouth shut!

Chris reached into his pocket.

Throw it out the window, I begged silently. Or use that big mouth of yours to chew it up and swallow it.

If Miss Gaunt lays her bony hands on it, I'm in major trouble.

Chris held out the note. "This note, Miss Gaunt?" he asked timidly.

Thanks, Chris, I thought. Thanks a lot.

She snatched the note from him and read it carefully.

What if she recognizes my handwriting?

What if she realizes I wrote the note?

My mouth turned dry. I tried to swallow, but I couldn't. My hands began to shake so I hid them under my desk.

"A ghost," Miss Gaunt announced slowly. "Someone has accused *me* of being a ghost!"

Miss Gaunt paced slowly up and down the aisles. Studying each kid in the class.

"Can you imagine why someone would say that about me, Tiffany?" she asked.

Tiffany opened her mouth, then shut it. She shook her head.

Even Tiffany couldn't speak. And she's never afraid to talk.

"Can you imagine such a thing, Ezra?"

Ezra shook his head, too. He stared down at his desk.

"Well, one of you imagined it," Miss Gaunt said, her little voice growing higher and louder. "Or you wouldn't have written such a thing in the first place!"

Miss Gaunt stopped at Debbie's desk. "Did you write the note, Debbie?" she asked.

"No, Miss Gaunt," Debbie mumbled.

"Can you imagine why someone would say that

75

I am a ghost?" Miss Gaunt asked. "Is it because I am not as young as I used to be?"

"I don't know, Miss Gaunt," Debbie said. "You don't look so old to me."

Yeah, right! I thought. Miss Gaunt is at least two hundred years old! Can't anyone else see that?

"Thank you, my dear." Miss Gaunt patted Debbie on the shoulder.

Debbie shivered.

Miss Gaunt proceeded down the next aisle.

She was closing in on me.

I checked the clock. Five minutes left to the end of class.

Miss Gaunt paused at Danny's desk.

"Is it because I wear white?" Miss Gaunt asked him. "Is *that* why I have been called a ghost?"

"Maybe," Danny said, shrugging.

"Do you think it's nice to call someone a ghost?" Miss Gaunt asked.

"I would *never* call anyone a ghost, Miss Gaunt," Danny said. "That's for sure."

"That's because you are a very sensitive person," she said as she glided across the room to the next aisle. "You would never be so unkind."

I glanced at the clock again.

Only three minutes left before the final bell.

Maybe she won't make it to me, I prayed.

76

"You can't imagine what it's like to be a substitute teacher," Miss Gaunt continued. "You hardly know a soul. You feel so alone. Then someone starts spreading unkind rumors." She spun around and glared at Bobby Dreyfuss. "How do you think that makes me feel?"

"Not good, I guess," Bobby answered, his lips quivering.

Miss Gaunt slammed her pointer down on his desk so hard he jumped out of his seat.

"Exactly!" Miss Gaunt screeched. "Let me tell you, boys and girls, gossip is not a pretty thing. Gossip is cruel. And what do we do to people who are cruel?"

Bobby stared up at her. "I-I guess we punish them," he stuttered.

"Punish them!" Miss Gaunt's voice grew even louder. "Very good, Bobby. That's exactly what we do. We punish them!"

I started to break out into a cold sweat. Tiny beads of perspiration dripped down my forehead.

If Miss Gaunt looks at me now, she'll know.

She'll know I wrote that note.

She'll know I said she was a ghost.

I checked the clock.

One minute left.

One minute until the bell.

77

"Don't worry, boys and girls," Miss Guant said, the tone of her voice suddenly soft and gentle. "I am not going to pursue this matter any further. I just want everyone to know that whoever wrote this note has hurt my feelings deeply. Very deeply."

The bell rang.

I could hardly believe my luck.

She didn't find out that I wrote the note!

I scooped up my backpack and raced to the door—and felt an icy hand squeeze my shoulder.

Miss Gaunt's hand.

"Zachariah," she said sweetly. "I am afraid I have to ask you to stay after class today!"

18

"But I-I've got to get home, Miss Gaunt," I stammered. "My mom's expecting me."

"This won't take but a moment, dear," she said.

A moment was way too long to be alone with a ghost.

But I didn't have any choice.

"Sorry," Chris mouthed on his way out the door.

Tiffany smiled sympathetically. But most of the other kids didn't even glance at me. They rushed out with their eyes glued to the floor.

When the last kid left, Miss Gaunt shut the

door. The quiet little click the lock made sent a chill down my spine.

Then she turned toward me. "You're frightened, aren't you, Zachariah?"

I nodded slowly.

"Lots of things scare you. Don't they, Zachariah?" she said. "That's why you bought that book *Power Kids,* isn't it?"

"N-no one knows about that," I stammered. "How could—"

"Oh, I noticed you in the bookstore," Miss Gaunt said. "It was the day before I started here. I visited town. To stretch my legs. And get the cobwebs out of my hair, so to speak. And I couldn't help thinking, 'What a fine boy. He'd be perfect.'"

Perfect for what? I wondered. *Perfect for what?*

"And here I was—just about to take over another class. But as soon as I spotted you, I knew I had to arrange for your teacher to come down with a cold. A nasty cold. It was naughty of me, I suppose, but I just couldn't resist!"

"Y-you made Miss Prescott sick?" I asked.

"I'm sorry to say I did. But I knew I *had* to be *your* teacher!"

Miss Gaunt approached her desk. She unfolded the note and read it again.

80

Maybe I can tell her the note was a joke, I thought. A stupid Halloween joke.

No. There's no way she'd believe me.

"What can I say, Zachariah?" Miss Gaunt asked. "Except that today I am very disappointed in you."

I was trapped!

And scared.

Really scared.

What was Miss Gaunt going to do to me?

She continued on. "You need to work on your spelling, dear." She held the note up in front of me. *"Careful* has only one *l.* Fortunately for you, your error won't influence your final grade."

Spelling! She wanted to talk to me about spelling?

"You're right, Miss Gaunt," I said quickly. "I'll go straight home and start studying."

"That won't be necessary, Zachariah."

Keep her talking, I told myself. Maybe Chris will wonder what's taking me so long. And he'll come back.

"Um. Is that how you knew I wrote the note?" I asked. "Because of the spelling?"

"Not entirely," Miss Gaunt said. "You followed me to the cemetery yesterday. You discovered the

81

grave—and the truth. So you see—you were the only one who could have written that note."

"Marcy could have!" I blurted.

"Well, we don't have to worry about her anymore. Do we?"

"What did you do to her?" I croaked. I was so frightened now, I nearly choked on my own words. "Where—where is she?"

"You know, Zachariah, I do not understand why you had to drag her along. She could have ruined everything."

I glanced behind me. Could I jump through one of the windows? I wondered.

Miss Gaunt placed the note on her desk and reached into a drawer. She lifted out a silver-wrapped box, topped with a shiny black bow.

"Ah!" she cried. "Enough about Marcy. I have a present for you."

What would a ghost give as a present? I didn't want to find out.

"That's okay, Miss Gaunt. You don't have to give me anything."

Could I push past her and escape?

"Nonsense, Zachariah," Miss Gaunt replied. "I want to give you a present. After all, *you* are my favorite student."

"What about Debbie Steinford?" The words

flew out of my mouth. "All the teachers love Debbie!"

"No. No. Zachariah. This is for you. To open later."

She shoved the package into my backpack. I didn't know what was in it—and I didn't want to know.

Miss Gaunt scooped up the note from her desk. She tore it up and threw the shreds in the wastebasket.

"No one believed your silly note," she said. "Which is certainly a nice piece of luck for me. I suspect the principal wouldn't be very happy if he knew I was a ghost!"

"I promise I won't tell anyone. You're a wonderful teacher, Miss Gaunt. I won't do anything to get you in trouble!"

Miss Gaunt smiled at me. "Do you really think I am a wonderful teacher, Zachariah?"

"Definitely. I've learned tons from you," I told her.

"Yes. You are correct. I am a wonderful teacher. And it's just not fair," Miss Gaunt said. "Can you imagine that I can leave my grave only once every ten years—the week before Halloween? That's not very often, is it?"

"No, Miss Gaunt," I agreed. "That's not very often."

How was I going to escape? I had to find a way out!

"And what's worse," she continued, "is that on the stroke of twelve on Halloween night I must return to my grave. Which is why I try to make the most of my time. I love every second of it, too. But especially the Halloween party. Do you like Halloween parties, Zachariah?"

"Oh, sure, Miss Gaunt," I answered nervously. "Who doesn't like Halloween parties?"

If I ran for it, would she try to catch me?

"Do you know what the highlight of the party is for me?" she asked.

I shook my head.

"The highlight is when I pick my favorite student," she said.

"What do you pick a student for?" My voice cracked.

"You know, don't you?" Miss Gaunt said. "That's why you're so frightened, isn't it?"

"I don't know anything. I don't know what you want with me. I don't want to know, Miss Gaunt. Please, let me go home," I begged.

She's never going to let me leave!

"Allow me to explain," Miss Gaunt began.

84

"Every ten years I select one student to take back with me," she said.

"Back with you?" I gasped. "Back where?"

"Why, back to the grave, of course," she said. "Back to the grave—to become a ghost like me. And then I will be able to teach them—forever!"

"I don't want to go with you, Miss Gaunt! I want to stay here in Shadyside!"

"But I need you, Zachariah," she said. "You're so much brighter than the others."

"I am not brighter," I protested. "I'm not good at decimals. I'm not good at spelling. You just said so yourself!"

"Ah, but you guessed what other children couldn't even imagine about me."

"No!" I shouted. "I won't go!"

"Oh, Zachariah." Miss Gaunt pouted. "Aren't you even a tiny bit pleased?"

I didn't trust myself to speak. I was afraid if I opened my mouth I would start screaming. And never stop.

I ran to the door.

I twisted the lock.

As I swung the door open, Miss Gaunt called after me. "Halloween . . . tomorrow, Zachariah. Midnight! To join our dark, dark world—of ghosts."

85

19

Her grave!

She's planning to take me back to her grave!

And make me a ghost!

I ran from the classroom.

I pounded down the hall. I slammed through the school's big double doors. And jumped off the top step, flying to the ground. Then I raced down Hawthorne as fast as I could.

The white strips of cloth hanging from the oak tree on the corner whipped across my face. I didn't slow down.

Jack-o'-lanterns leered at my from every porch.

Jack-o'-lanterns for Halloween.

I slipped on some wet leaves and nearly fell.

Don't stop, I told myself. Just get home. Get home and don't come out until Halloween is over.

I ran so hard I thought my chest would explode.

Home, I thought every time one of my feet hit the cement.

Home, home, home, home.

I turned a corner. I was nearly there!

I dashed past the neighbors' houses. Then I cut across my lawn and charged up to the door.

It was locked.

I shoved my hands into my pockets. Empty. What did I do with my key?

I hammered on the door. "Let me in!" I screamed.

What if Miss Gaunt realizes I'm never coming out of the house? What if she's on her way here? What if she decides to take me back to her grave—now?

I beat on the door with both fists.

"Who is it?" I heard my brother, Kevin, call in a high voice.

"Kevin, let me in!" I hollered.

"We don't need anything. Have a nice day!" Kevin trilled.

"Kevin, open it! Now! Or I'm calling Mom!"

"Mom's not home!" Kevin yelled back.

I rammed my shoulder against the door the way they do in cop shows. I didn't care if I broke the door down. I had to get inside.

I threw myself at the door again. And as I did, Kevin opened it. I soared into the hallway.

Kevin laughed like an idiot.

I slammed the door and locked it. I slid the chain in place.

Kevin leaned against the wall. Watching. "I knew Halloween would drive you completely insane some year," he told me.

I ignored him. I ran around to the back door and locked it. Then I made sure every window was locked.

Are ghosts like vampires? I wondered. Do they have to be invited in before they can enter a house?

I hurried upstairs and checked all the windows up there, too. I triple-checked my own window. Then I threw myself facedown on my bed.

My backpack opened and something slid out.

Miss Gaunt's present.

I threw it on the floor.

And stared at it.

Miss Gaunt had wrapped it carefully. The corners were nice and smooth. The black bow was arranged just so.

What is in it? I wondered. Some gross dead thing? Or something worse? Something alive? Is it safe to have it in the house?

I sat up and nudged the present with my toe. I didn't hear anything. I gave the package a kick. Nothing.

I knelt down and ran my fingers over the silver paper. It felt like a book.

I slowly tore away a corner of the paper. I was right. A book.

I inhaled deeply.

A book.

That's not so bad.

I ripped the rest of the paper away.

My stomach lurched when I read the front cover.

The title said: *The Book of the Dead.*

20

*T*he Book of the Dead.

I touched the cover with the tip of one finger. I expected it to feel cold—like Miss Gaunt.

But it didn't. It felt warm.

I opened it up—and spotted my name! I slammed the book shut.

I'm throwing this thing out, I decided. There's nothing in *The Book of the Dead* that I need to know. At least not for a long, *long* time.

I grabbed the book and tossed it in the wastebasket.

Wait, I thought. Maybe I should read the part that has my name in it.

I flipped open the cover. It was an inscription and it said:

> For Zachariah,
> Welcome!
> Your teacher *forever*,
> Evangeline Gaunt.

No way, I thought. No way!

I noticed again how warm the book felt. It started to pulse under my fingertips. As if it were alive.

I flung it back into the trash.

Don't flip out, I told myself. Don't flip out. You just have to make it through one more day. At midnight on Halloween this will all be over.

I headed back downstairs. Usually I avoid Kevin—especially when Mom and Dad aren't around to referee. But I was terrified, and I didn't want to be by myself.

Chris called on the phone about a million times, but I made Kevin tell him I wasn't feeling well.

After dinner I hung around my parents. It would be pretty hard for Miss Gaunt to drag me away from them, I figured. I could tell my parents thought I was acting weird, but they didn't say anything about it.

After my favorite TV show ended, Mom said it was time for bed.

Sleep. Upstairs. Alone.

"Can't I stay up a little bit longer?" I begged.

"Sorry, Zach," she replied. "You know it's a school night."

I practically crawled up the stairs. But when I reached my room, I sprinted inside and jumped between the sheets of my bed. Then I tugged the covers up to my chin.

Every time I closed my eyes, I imagined myself lying in a grave. With thousands of swollen worms wriggling underneath me.

So I stayed up all night.

Trying to come up with a plan.

A plan to stay home from school.

My life depended on it!

The next morning I leaped out of bed.

I slipped into the bathroom and closed the door. I turned on the hot water in the bathtub and let it run. I wanted the bathroom to be nice and steamy.

After about five minutes my pajamas began to stick to me. Now I appeared all sweaty.

I drenched a washcloth in hot tap water, and I wrung it out. Then I pressed it to my forehead. Instant fever!

I bolted downstairs before my fake fever cooled.

"You'd better get dressed, honey," Mom said as I entered the kitchen. "You don't want to be late for school."

Yes, I do, I thought. I want to be so late that I won't arrive there till tomorrow.

She held out a glass of orange juice. I pushed it away. I sagged into my chair. "I don't feel so well," I moaned.

Kevin wandered in and plopped down across the table. He snagged my juice.

Mom placed her hand on my forehead. "You do feel a little warm," she commented.

"Check his pulse," Kevin said. "Just to see if he has one."

"Be nice," Mom said. "Your poor brother isn't feeling well. You go back to bed, honey. I'll bring you something to eat in a few minutes."

Before Mom started talking about calling the doctor, I darted upstairs. I turned on the TV and tuned into some lame game shows.

But I watched the clock more than I watched the television—counting down the time until I was safe from Miss Gaunt.

At four o'clock I couldn't decide whether I should be relieved—or more scared than ever. The

93

Halloween party was over. But it was hours until midnight.

And now that school was out, Miss Gaunt could be anywhere. I had eight more hours to go. Eight long hours.

The next two hours I didn't even pretend to watch TV. I stared at the clock. Gazing at the seconds and minutes ticking away.

Mom popped into my room at six o'clock. She felt my forehead. "Good!" she exclaimed. No more fever! Are you ready for Halloween?" she asked.

I nearly gasped. "I-uh-thought I wasn't allowed out today."

"Wouldn't you like to greet the trick-or-treaters at the door?"

"Oh, sure," I answered. Boy, was I relieved.

"Great costume, Zack," Kevin called as I came down the stairs.

"I'm not wearing a costume," I snapped.

"Sure you are. You're the Big Pain!" Kevin laughed. "You'll do anything to get out of Halloween, won't you?" he demanded. "You can fool Mom, but you can't fool me."

I ignored him. He shuffled off to the kitchen.

The doorbell rang.

I grabbed the bowl of candy Mom had set out on the hall table.

I pulled open the door.

"Trick or treat! Trick or treat!"

A bunch of little kids perched on the porch. I could see their mothers waiting for them on the sidewalk. I dropped candy in each of their bags.

The doorbell rang again.

"Trick or treat! Trick or treat!"

A Martian, a dinosaur, and a ballerina appeared.

I handed out the candy—and even pretended to be frightened of the tiny dinosaur. The kids giggled as I closed the door.

The doorbell rang again.

It's going to be a busy night, I thought. Halloween will be over before I know it!

I opened the door.

Only one person stood there.

"Trick or treat, Zachariah!"

Miss Gaunt!

21

I froze in the doorway. I stared at the white gauzy gown. The white gloves. The veil.

It was Miss Gaunt! She had come for me!

"You can't come in!" I shouted. "I won't let you."

"Zack, honey?" Mom ran in from the kitchen. "Is everything okay?"

I clutched Mom's arm. "It's Miss Gaunt. My substitute teacher!" I cried. "Don't let her take me away!"

"Let me feel your forehead," Mom said. "Maybe you do have a fever."

"She wants to kidnap me!" I screamed as Mom lifted her hand to my forehead. "She is going to kill me and make me live in the graveyard!"

"But, Zack—" Mom started.

"Save me, Mom," I interrupted. "You've got to save me!"

"But, Zack," Mom said again. "Miss Gaunt isn't here. It's just . . ."

Then I heard the laughter. I turned. Miss Gaunt had lifted her veil. And underneath—it wasn't Miss Gaunt at all.

It was Chris. And now he was doubled over, laughing his head off.

"Did I really look like her?" Chris asked between gasps of laughter.

"You know you look *exactly* like her!" I said. "You did this on purpose. Just to scare me!"

"I thought it would be funny," Chris said, still chuckling. "Besides, I didn't come over just to scare you. I came to see how you were feeling."

"Why, isn't that nice of him?" Mom said. "Would you like a treat, Chris?"

"Thanks, Mrs. Pepper," Chris said. He strolled over to the treat table. Once Mom headed back to the kitchen, he started cramming candy bars into his pillowcase.

"Anyone notice I was sick?" I asked Chris. "Besides you, I mean?"

"Miss Gaunt noticed. And boy, did she seem upset. She really *is* nuts about you."

"Upset how?" I asked. "Was she, um, sad-upset—or angry-upset?"

"More like brokenhearted-upset," Chris said. "I have to admit, it was a little weird."

Chris shook his pillowcase to make room for more candy. Then he continued. "Anyway, Miss Gaunt told us that Miss Prescott will be back on Monday. Miss Gaunt said she was really sorry to leave without saying goodbye to you and Marcy."

"Has anybody heard from Marcy?" I asked anxiously.

"Nah. But I passed her house coming here. The window is fixed. I'm sure she'll be home soon."

That's what you think, I muttered under my breath.

"What?" Chris asked. His pillowcase was full now, and he was getting ready to leave.

I knew Chris would never believe me. But I had to try to convince him. "Miss Gaunt is a ghost!" I shouted. "And she's done something horrible to Marcy and her family."

"Oh, right," Chris said sarcastically. "I read your stupid note."

"She really is a ghost. And she got rid of Marcy because we saw her grave."

"What grave?"

"Her grave. Miss Gaunt's grave! It said 'Born 1769. Died 1845.'"

"You saw *her* grave?" Chris asked. "With her name on it?"

"Yes!" I answered with a sigh of relief. It looked as if Chris was finally beginning to believe me.

Chris set his pillowcase on the floor. "Hmmm. I know. It was probably her great-great-great grandmother's grave."

"But the grave was empty!" I cried.

"That doesn't prove she's a ghost, Zack."

"Look, Chris. Marcy's gone. Gone because we saw Miss Gaunt's grave. Because we know the truth. Miss Gaunt is a ghost. Why won't you believe me? She told me that she wants to take me back with her to the graveyard. Tonight. Why would she say that if she weren't a ghost?"

"For special math tutoring?" Chris asked, starting to laugh again.

"No! NO! NO!" I screamed. "She wants to turn me into a ghost, too."

"Well, maybe you won't be afraid of ghosts anymore—once you're one of them." Chris laughed so hard now he had to clutch his sides.

"What's all the laughing about?" Mom asked, coming up beside me. "Are you feeling better?"

"No, Mom. I'm not feeling better. In fact, I feel a lot worse," I said, glaring at Chris.

"Well, why don't you go up to bed?" Mom replied. "Get some rest. I have to go next door for a few minutes. Come on, Chris. I'll walk you out."

Chris and Mom left. I practically slammed the door behind them. I noticed Chris's pillowcase on the floor. He had left it behind. Well, too bad. He wasn't getting it back.

I started up the stairs to bed when the doorbell rang again. "Kevin!" I yelled for my brother. "Get the door!"

No answer.

Great. I muttered. Kevin never does anything around here. I'll be answering the door all night.

The doorbell rang again.

"Okay. Okay. I'm coming."

As I approached the door, I could hear the shouts of the trick-or-treaters outside. I wished Halloween were over.

I yanked the door open. It was Chris.

"Forget it! I'm not giving you your stupid candy!" I shouted.

"Candy? I didn't come for candy, Zachariah. I came for you!"

It was Miss Gaunt.

The real Miss Gaunt!

22

Miss Gaunt reached out a gloved hand and grasped me tightly by the wrist.

"No!" I shrieked. "I won't go! I don't want to be a ghost!"

"It doesn't matter what you want!" she said calmly. "Don't you understand that?"

She didn't sound like an old lady anymore. Her voice was strong—and mean. And her grip was like iron.

She yanked me forward, dragging me toward the front door. I grabbed the doorknob to the front closet. I tried to pull myself back.

"Help!" I screamed. "Help!"

I heard footsteps coming down the stairs. Kevin.

As soon as he appeared, Miss Gaunt loosened her grip. "Hello, there," Miss Gaunt said. "I'm Zachariah's substitute teacher. I stopped by to invite him to a Halloween party."

"Don't believe her!" I cried. "Our class Halloween party was this afternoon!"

Kevin studied Miss Gaunt. "Hey, that's a really cool costume," he finally said. Then he turned to me. "Zack, you're pathetic. You'd say anything to skip Halloween."

"Actually, Zack is right. Our class Halloween party was this afternoon," Miss Gaunt said sweetly. "But some of the children thought it would be nice to have another one tonight. It would be a shame for Zack to miss that one, too."

"Don't let her take me!" I shrieked. "She's going to force me into the graveyard and turn me into a ghost—just like her!"

"Are you really going to turn Zack into a ghost?" Kevin laughed.

"I promised him I would," Miss Gaunt said. "I think it's important for grown-ups to live up to their promises. Don't you?"

"Well, have a great time at the party," Kevin said, heading up the stairs.

I tried to run after him, but Miss Gaunt was way too fast for me. She lunged for my arm. Her grip felt strong enough to crush my bones.

She jerked me down our front path onto the sidewalk. As we passed our neighbor's house, I screamed. "Mom! Come out! Mom!" But she couldn't hear me.

My shoes scraped the sidewalk as Miss Gaunt yanked on my arm. I thought she was going to pull it right out of its socket.

My eyes searched the street for help. Two kids dressed as aliens were approaching us.

"Help! Help!" I screamed.

"Oooh! Oooh!" they giggled.

"She's going to turn me into a ghost!" I cried.

"Really?" one of the aliens asked.

"I'm certainly going to do my best," Miss Gaunt replied in her thin, breathy voice.

The kids laughed and jogged up the steps to the next house.

Miss Gaunt gripped my arm tighter. Practically lifting me off the ground. We glided down the street.

"Help me!" I begged two masked bandits. "She's kidnapping me!"

But the bandits laughed, too.

We turned down Fear Street.

There were no trick-or-treaters. No one out. The street was deserted. The air—perfectly still. Nothing moved.

A dim light shone through the window of a house every now and then. But mostly it was dark. And creepy. As creepy as the night Marcy and I followed Miss Gaunt on our bikes.

"Miss Gaunt, please don't do this. Please," I begged, struggling to free myself.

"But I have to, Zachariah," Miss Gaunt answered. "You're such a good student. I want to teach you—forever."

I tried to rip my arm from Miss Gaunt's grasp. She clamped down harder. Nothing could stop her. She glided faster down Fear Street, dragging me behind.

We reached a corner. And turned.

We had come to the Fear Street Cemetery.

"Home, Zachariah," Miss Gaunt announced. "Home at last!"

23

"**N**o way!" I screamed. "I'm not going in there. You're never going to get away with this!"

"But I already have!" she cackled.

I twisted in Miss Gaunt's grip. But she had the strength of a wrestler.

I opened my mouth wide and sank my teeth into the folds of her gauzy sleeve. I heard a sickening crunch. Her arm snapped. I had broken her bone. In the moonlight I glimpsed the jagged edge poking through her sleeve. But it didn't seem to matter. Her grip was as strong as ever.

"Don't do that again," Miss Gaunt warned.

"You don't want to make me cross, do you, Zachariah?"

We entered the Fear Street Cemetery. And I spotted a familiar-looking man. It was Mr. Sangfwad from Shop Till You Drop (Dead!).

What was he doing in the cemetery? Could he save me?

"Mr. Sangfwad!" I yelled. "Help me! Mr. Sangfwad!"

Mr. Sangfwad turned toward me. But he made no effort to help. He didn't seem to recognize me.

"It's me!" I screamed. "Zack Pepper. I was in your store the other day."

"Ah," he said as he moved closer. And then I realized why Mr. Sangfwad didn't know who I was. His eyes were gone! Two empty sockets stared out into the darkness.

Mr. Sangfwad was a ghost, too!

"Welcome to our little party," he said. Then he wiped some drool from his bony chin.

"Let me go," I begged. "I want to go home."

"But the party's just begun," Miss Gaunt crooned.

"I don't want to be at this party!" I cried out. "I don't belong here."

"But you're the life of the party!" Mr. Sangfwad cackled. "At least until midnight."

"Wh-what happens at midnight?" I asked.

Mr. Sangfwad placed his face close to mine. I tried to shrink back from his foul breath. But Miss Gaunt held me firmly.

His lips brushed my ear as he whispered into it. "At midnight you will become the un-life of the party. You will turn into a ghost—just like us."

Then Mr. Sangfwad threw back his head and shrieked—like a madman.

"I don't want to be a ghost!" I cried over his awful howls.

"I am afraid Zachariah isn't in a party mood tonight," Miss Gaunt said. "It was nice to see you, Mr. Sangfwad. But we must be on our way."

Miss Gaunt tugged me deeper into the grave-yard. But we could still hear Mr. Sangfwad's shrieks echoing all around us.

The air grew colder as we plunged deeper still. The graves in this part of the cemetery were older and smaller. I tried to focus on them, but we were moving too fast. They passed in a blur.

And then, finally, we stopped.

At a grave.

The open grave Marcy and I had seen before.

Only this time, a coffin rested within it.

And the lid was open. Waiting.

Waiting for us.

24

*"Y*ou can't make me go down there," I screeched. "I won't let you!"

"Oh, Zachariah," Miss Gaunt said. "It's no use fighting. Can't you see that?"

"But I don't want to go with you!" I pleaded. "I want to go home."

"But this *is* your home," Miss Gaunt said. "Come, Zachariah. It is time."

"No!" I screamed. "I won't! I can't!"

I pushed back with all my strength. The force set me free! My head hit the ground with a thud. Right next to the open grave.

I gazed up. Miss Gaunt was calmly peeling off one of her white gloves.

I inched my way back. Back. Sliding along the wet grass.

Miss Gaunt moved forward. Slowly. Then her arm shot out. And before I could dodge away, her bare bony fingers were digging deep into my shoulder.

She lifted me up with one hand. "Come with me, Zachariah," she whispered.

My strength faded. My legs began to tremble. Step by step, my feet slipped across the grass as Miss Gaunt pulled me forward.

I hovered at the edge of the grave now. Peering down. Down at the open coffin.

Miss Gaunt stood beside me. "Welcome home, Zachariah," she said, with a soft cackle. And then she shoved me. One quick hard shove.

And before I knew it, I was falling.

Falling into Miss Gaunt's grave.

Into the open coffin.

25

~~~~~

"**H**elp!" I screamed. "Help!"

I landed facedown in the coffin.

"Comfy, isn't it?" Miss Gaunt purred from above.

I scrambled to my feet. I threw myself against the side of the grave, struggling to climb out. I clutched at the dirt—trying to pull myself up. But the ancient soil crumbled beneath my grip.

"Help!" I screamed again. "Someone, help me!"

"My goodness, Zachariah," Miss Gaunt said. "Please. Not so loud. You're going to wake up the dead." And then she laughed. Not her wispy laugh—a deep, cruel laugh.

I reached up. Groping at the wall of the grave. My fingers wrapped around a thick tree root. I dug my hands into the dirt and grasped the root tightly. I began to hoist myself out.

"Save your strength," Miss Gaunt called down. "You can't escape. It's much too late for that. It's almost midnight."

"No!" I cried out. "I'm not staying here with you!"

"I'm afraid you have no choice, dear," she said, kneeling beside the grave, peering down. "Just think how lovely it's going to be. Think of all the time we'll have together. All the things I'll be able to teach you. After all, I am a wonderful teacher."

I reached up—to shove Miss Gaunt back. But my hand caught her veil—ripping it away.

"What have you done?" Miss Gaunt shrieked. She jerked up and turned to search the ground for her veil.

I clutched the tree root tightly. I jammed one foot into the dirt. Then I pushed up with the other foot with all my strength.

I sprang up.

I held on to the tree root with one hand and reached out for the grave's opening with the other. Then I pulled myself out.

113

I jumped quickly to my feet.

Miss Gaunt whirled around.

And her face was gone!

No flesh.

Just a bony skull holding a few wisps of gray hair. And worms. Slimy purple worms. Crawling in and out of the sockets where her eyes should have been.

I choked back a scream. My hands flew to my eyes, covering them.

"Look at me, Zachariah," Miss Gaunt ordered.

"I can't!" I shrieked, gasping for breath.

"You must," she commanded harshly. Then her voice softened. "You must, Zachariah. You must. Because in a few minutes, you will look exactly like this, too."

My hands floated away from my eyes. Moving by themselves—controlled by Miss Gaunt. I stared into her horrifying face.

"You can't get away from me!" she said. "I'm never going to let you go. Never!"

I glanced down at her hands. Her raw, bony fingers twitched in the moonlight.

Then they shot out and curled around my neck.

"Let me go!" I shrieked. I tried to pry her fingers from my throat, but she was too strong.

I struggled hard. She shoved me back. My foot

114

dangled over the open grave. I was losing my balance.

In the distance the town clock began to strike midnight. One . . . Two . . . Three . . .

Footsteps. It was difficult to tell, but I thought I heard footsteps.

Miss Gaunt heard them, too.

She snapped her head up. She peered over my shoulder. Her body stiffened.

She lifted a bony finger and pointed. "Wh-who is . . ."

What could possibly scare *her* this much?

I whirled around.

It was another Miss Gaunt!

26

Another Miss Gaunt—with big white high-tops peeking out from under her white dress. Chris!

I was never so glad to see him in my life!

"Come on! Help me!" I cried out. I grabbed Miss Gaunt's spindly arm and swung her into the coffin.

Then I slammed the lid down and jumped on top of the coffin. It rumbled underneath me.

"Come on, Chris! Help me hold this thing down, now!"

The clock continued to chime. Seven . . . Eight . . .

Chris jumped down next to me. His "Miss

Gaunt" veil flew up in his face as the wind began to blow. Then the whole ground shook.

The coffin lid jerked open and a howling wind escaped from inside the casket!

We slammed the lid down again. It snapped open once more—with a force that sent dirt flinging from the grave.

"Hold it down!" I screamed. "Hold it down!"

Nine . . .

The wind howled in our ears. Soil and rocks whipped around us. Pelting us.

There were only seconds left until midnight. Seconds before Miss Gaunt returned to the world of ghosts. Seconds before I was safe—finally.

Ten . . .

The coffin lid wrenched open and a bony hand shot out! It grabbed me by the ankle.

"Oh, no! Not now!" I shrieked. I kicked wildly to free myself—before it was too late. But the harder I struggled, the tighter her grip grew.

Eleven . . .

I was slipping—slipping into the coffin. Slipping away—forever.

Twelve!

A jagged bolt of lightning sliced through the sky. It pierced the ground next to the grave.

Miss Gaunt's bony hand suddenly dropped

from my leg. I watched in horror as it shriveled up and shrank back into the coffin.

Then the wind died. And the dirt storm settled.

The cemetery grew silent.

It was midnight. Halloween had ended.

I didn't realize I had been holding my breath. I let out a long sigh.

Chris and I pulled ourselves out of the grave.

"Thanks," I said, turning toward him. The color had completely drained from his face. Even his freckles were pale.

"I-I was walking by the cemetery," he stammered. "I heard someone screaming for help. It sounded like you."

"You showed up just in time!" I cried.

"I-I can't believe it," he said. "Miss Gaunt really was a ghost!"

Even in the moonlight, there was no mistaking the look on Chris's face. The look of horror. For the first time all week, I smiled.

27

"**I** decided to let you sleep in," Mom said when I walked into the kitchen Saturday morning. "I was afraid you didn't get enough sleep last night."

"I feel terrific, Mom," I said, chugging my juice.

"Well, I don't approve of your teacher keeping you out that late," Mom said. "And I'm going to talk to her about it."

"I don't think you can," I said. "Yesterday was her last day."

"I'll find her number in the telephone book," Mom replied. "What is her last name? Gaunt. Right?"

"Uh-huh," I said. "But I have a feeling her number is unlisted."

I grabbed a piece of toast and headed for the door. "See you later."

I raced over to Marcy's house. The window was fixed, but the house appeared deserted. I knocked on the door.

It slowly creaked open. And there she was!

"Marcy!" I cried. "You're here!"

Marcy stepped outside. She closed the door behind her very carefully. "Dad said not to slam the door," Marcy explained. "That's how he broke the window the other day."

Well, that explains one thing, I thought.

"Marcy, where *were* you?" I asked.

We sat on her front lawn. "It was the weirdest thing," she began. "After you rode off Thursday, I ran into the house. And Mom was on the phone. When she hung up she said we had to leave for my grandmother's house upstate right away."

"Did she say why?" I asked.

"Yes. She said Grandma was very sick."

"What's weird about that?" I asked.

"Wait," Marcy said, holding up her hand. Then she continued. "We jumped in the car. Dad drove all night. We reached Grandma's house Friday morning. Grandma ran out of the house to meet us. And she was fine!"

"Pretty fast recovery, huh?" I said.

"No, Zack. *That* was the weird part. Grandma said she never called. She didn't know what Mom was talking about."

"I bet Miss Gaunt did it!" I cried. Then I told Marcy all about Halloween.

Marcy couldn't believe what had happened. "Well, at least no one will ever tease you about ghosts again."

"Yeah," I agreed. Then I jumped up. "Hey, there's Chris!" I waved him over.

"Chris, I was just telling Marcy all about Halloween."

"What about it?" Chris said.

Chris was playing it cool. I guess he couldn't bear the thought that I was right for once.

"Oh, just about Miss Gaunt being a ghost and all."

"Miss Gaunt? A ghost? Are you starting that again?"

"What do you mean?" I shouted in Chris's face. "Of course Miss Gaunt was a ghost. You saw her. You were in the cemetery with me! You were scared to death!"

Chris laughed. "Me? Scared? No way. That ghost stuff is strictly in *your* dreams, Zack. Not mine."

Chris didn't remember a thing. It was the last of Miss Gaunt's ghostly magic.

On Monday morning I walked to school by myself. When the school came into view, I reached into my backpack and pulled out Chris's snake. It was hard to believe—only a couple of weeks ago this thing terrified me.

I held the snake to my face and felt its slimy texture on my skin.

"Oshee ma terr hoom," I chanted softly. "Kubal den skaya!" It was one of the chants I had memorized from the book I rescued from the garbage—*The Book of the Dead.*

The rubber snake came to life. It slithered through my fingers. I patted it gently.

"So, Chris isn't scared of anything," I said to myself. "We'll see."

I ran up the stairs to Shadyside Middle School and raced down the hall. I learned a lot from Miss Gaunt, I thought as the snake slithered happily down into my backpack. Miss Gaunt was a wonderful teacher.